the PHANTOM DETECTIVE

Volume Two

AIRSHIP 27 PRODUCTIONS

TM

The Phantom Detective Volume Two

"The Zeppelin Zombies From Zurich" ©2023 Carson Demmans
"Doorway to Hell" ©2023 Gene Moyers
"The Master Youths of Janus" ©2023 Michael F. Housel
"Nine of Your Best Friends" ©2023 Fred Adams Jr.

Published by Airship 27 Productions
www.airship27.com
www.airship27hangar.com

Cover © 2023 Adam Shaw
Interior illustrations © 2023 Kevin Broden

Editor: Ron Fortier
Associate Editor: Jay Sweet
Marketing and Promotions Manager: Michael Vance
Production and design by Rob Davis

ISBN: 978-1-953589-62-0

Printed in the United States of America

10 9 8 7 6 5 4 3 2 1

Volume Two

Table of Contents

THE ZEPPELIN ZOMIBIES FROM ZURICH

by Carson Demmans

It was a simple patch of grass on an unremarkable field. Even in the dim moonlight in the middle of July, 1934, it appeared to be nothing more and nothing less. There were no spooky shadows playing across it that might be goblins and no hidden holes that a man might fall into.

Still, this patch of land terrified Homer Ludquist more than if he had seen Satan himself playing croquet on it. Homer did not believe in Satan, so if he saw him, Homer would know it was not real.

But it was on this patch of land, 80 years previously to the day, Orion Williamson had disappeared in broad daylight. Everyone had warned Homer of the legend when he bought the cursed piece of land. He was glad for the legend then, because that was why he was able to buy the parcel that contained this jinxed portion so cheaply. But now it scared him.

He had planned to come to this area in the middle of the day at the same time Orion, a local farmer just like Homer, had disappeared, but had lost his nerve at the last second. He decided to come at night and alone instead. If he lost his nerve again, there would be no witnesses, and he could brag about it later that he had the courage to come to cursed land at the witching hour.

"Maybe witnesses would have been better," Homer thought to himself. It was a strange thought to have when fighting for his life, but what is the proper thing to think at that time?

He had been standing there, scratching his head at the pure normalcy of the feared piece of grass and dirt when something dropped on him from above. He soon realized that it was actually several somethings, and they were all desperately trying to get a grip on him. The sheer number of them protected him momentarily as they crowded each other out on his limited amount of skin.

He tried to turn his head but it was a pointless exercise as something was wrapped around his face to the point he couldn't see even if he could turn his head. His arms were weighted down with something that prevented him from moving them.

But they weren't just weighted, he realized. They were being actively pulled down, and it wasn't just one thing wrapped around his arms, it was many.

Fingers! From the tips of his fingernails to his shoulders, his strong arms were beings crushed by the fingers of many men. Individually, their grips felt weak, but with ten or more hands on each arm, he was no match for them.

Terrified of the memory that the body of Orion Williamson had never been found despite more than seventy-five years of searching, Homer continued to fight. He strained and struggled. Beads of sweat turned into rivers of perspiration, his skin covered with one giant oil slick. One grasping hand slipped off his right arm, and then another. With less opposition, his right arm broke free and he pried his mysterious blindfold off his face. When he succeeded in doing so, he was staring face to face with a cadaverous madman who was so thin that his body had made a good substitute for a strong piece of cloth. His eyes bulged from his sockets to the point that Homer feared that they would explode. Homer only realized that the man was not actually a corpse when it burst into incoherent laughter, which was soon joined in by the blindfold man's allies.

"At least they're human," Homer thought. Like all men, he feared the unknown, but knowing that his attackers were as human as he was, and in considerably worse physical condition gave him a glimmer of hope. Years of physical farm labor had left him as strong as an ox and able to work all day without stopping, He began prying more of his deathly thin attackers off of himself when he went blind again.

"But that's impossible!" He thought. The blindfold man was at least six feet away from Homer the last time he had seen him a split second ago. He was being pulled down again, but this time it really was by weight. His attackers had given up on trying to out muscle their opponent and now relied on sheer weight of numbers. Homer could feel man after man drop on top of him. His legs were released, but it did him no good. He tried to kick with his right leg, but his left leg was too weak to support the growing mass and he soon fell to the ground as his leg buckled. His collapse threw some of his attackers off of him, but they were being replaced and added to at an increasing rate.

Homer had not led a virtuous life. He had drank, smoked, gambled. He had abandoned God and religion at an early age. He had enjoyed beating up those smaller than him, cheated on his wife, cheated men out of money. Maybe he had been wrong. Maybe there was a God. But if so, why was He emptying a giant salt shaker full of skinny lunatics on his head? Which of his crimes deserved such a strange punishment?

He could hear moans now. Some of his attackers were having their frail bodies crushed as their comrades fell on top of them from some unknown height. Homer was built far more sturdily than his unknown foes. It was a long shot, but maybe they would disable enough of each other that he would be able to power his way out of the situation. He drew his arms back and his legs forward so he was in a "turtle" position. With his strong legs now underneath a portion of his upper body, he drove himself upward as hard as he could and regained a standing position. His attackers surrounded him, but they did nothing but stare at him in anticipation, but the anticipation of what?

It was then that Homer realized that a noose had been slipped around his neck while his enemies had swarmed over him. It quickly tightened as many hands pulled on it from above. He grabbed the rope with both hand and pulled down on it as hard as he could to create enough slack so he would not be strangled. But, the unseen men weren't trying to choke him. They were lifting him off the ground!

Kicking with both legs now, Homer attempted a scream, but his throat was under too much pressure to emit any sound. His kicking made him spin around as he was hauled up into thin air. For the first time he saw that he had been attacked by twenty men, all as emaciated and demented as the blindfold man. Some seemed to be floating in the air and rising upwards, and others seemed to be almost swimming. As his eyes adjusted to the light, he realized that they were climbing or being hauled by black ropes, so that none of them were being left behind. Above him there was only blackness.

"I'm being pulled into a hole in the sky," Homer thought. He wasn't, of course, but it is also hard to think of something appropriate when you are being eaten alive by dozens of hungry mouths in a floating cave of darkness.

· · ·

Richard Curtis Van Loan sighed with relief as he saw a familiar red beacon on the New York sky line as he drove his sleek sports car as fast as traffic would allow. He was driving aimlessly around the city and happy to see the beacon for the same reason: he was bored. The beacon meant the Phantom was being called into action. The Phantom: crime fighter! The Phantom: adventurer! The Phantom: detective!

And Richard Curtis Van Loan was the Phantom!

The red beacon was the signal that his trusted friend, crusading newspaper publisher Frank Havens, one of the few people alive who knew that Van Loan was the Phantom, had been advised by one of the many reporters on one of his many newspapers that made a chain from coast to coast east and west and from border to border north and south, that trouble was afoot. And, not just any trouble! His reporters thought they were simply reporting the strangest crime stories they had come across that week to their boss. In reality, they were unknowingly acting as scouts for cases so strange and devious and that posed such a threat to mankind that only one man in the World could face them: The Phantom.

Instead of heading for Frank Havens' building, where the beacon was located, Van Loan immediately drove away from it in a casual manner. When he found a deserted alley, he parked in it. He took out his slim makeup kit and began to not just change his appearance, but to become a different person. He plumped his lips with a special cream and puffed out his cheeks with cotton swabs placed inside his mouth. Using putty, he changed the shape and color of his nose until it was so bulbous and red it would make W.C. Fields jealous.

Gone was the refined gentleman who was one of New York's most eligible bachelors. The man who drove out of the alley looked like a lifelong drunk, and not anyone that people would want to talk to willingly.

Now Van Loan headed towards the red beacon as fast as traffic would allow. He weaved in and out of traffic with ease, and many cars gladly moved out of his way when they saw his intoxicated looking appearance. Once he arrived at the building, he easily evaded the building's security and walked in unannounced into Frank Havens' office.

Havens had been an old friend of Van Loan's father and had known Van Loan for all of the younger man's life, but such was the skill of disguise of the Phantom that even Havens could not tell by appearance that his intruder was Van Loan, but he still knew it was.

"Hello Dick," Havens said warmly. "Only you could have penetrated my extra security forces so easily and without being caught."

The Phantom laughed at the joke but made a mental note that his incredible detective skills might actually reveal who he was if he used them while in disguise.

"Have you ever heard of Orion Williamson?" Havens asked as he shook Van Loan's hand.

"I've heard the legend," Van replied. "The man who disappeared into thin air."

"Ah," said Havens with a wide grin. "Then you don't know the real story. Scientists have examined the field that he disappeared from and declared it to be impossible. Historians say that there is no record of an Orion Williamson in Selma, Alabama at any time, let alone when he was supposed to have disappeared. But newspapermen know the true story!"

"But it's just a myth," Van Loan said dubiously. As the Phantom he had faced many strange menaces, but there had always been a scientific explanation to them. Despite his name, the Phantom did not believe in the supernatural. Alleged gods and monsters all turned out to be monsters of the human variety.

"No!" said Havens in a stern voice as he smacked his fist on his desk. "The scientists and historians were wrong. Orion Williamson was a real man. He had no birth certificate and never attended school, but he was real. Mrs. Williamson was interviewed and re-interviewed by the best newspapermen in the country, including my grandfather. He told me the story over and over again when I was a child. I insisted on it. I assure you that my grandfather was better at telling that someone was lying then the polygraph will ever be, and he swore she was telling the truth. On a clear sunny day, her husband was standing on solid ground one second and disappeared into thin air the next. He was never seen again, and every reporter in the country looked for him at one time or another. To solve this mystery would be the Holy Grail of journalism, and I am on the verge of finding it!"

"Is that the reason for the extra security?" the Phantom asked. There was at least triple the number of night watchman patrolling the building compared to other nights.

"Unfortunately, yes," Havens sighed. "My family has been in the newspaper business a long time, Dick. We have been involved in feuds that make the Hatfields and the Mc Coys look like a school yard fight between five year old girls. In this particular case, a competitor, Ned Johnson, published headlines in all of his papers fifty years ago that one of his reporters had found the skeleton of Orion Williamson. My father was instrumental in proving that it was a hoax. He never implied that Johnson was in on it, but that was what the public chose to believe. He committed suicide shortly thereafter and his daughter swore vengeance on me. She sold off the newspaper part of her father's business empire and concentrated on investing in the stock market instead. She is a very wealthy and powerful woman. Amelia Johnson is not a woman to be trifled with."

"Amelia Johnson?" the Phantom said with curiosity. "The explorer?"

"The same," Havens sighed. "Using a balloon, she has accessed some of the most remote places in the world. It was a trick she learned from her father. He did it as publicity stunts to sell newspapers, but she does it for the love of adventure. The one thing she does have in common with her late father however is an obsession with Orion Williamson. I have no doubt she would steal the secret from me and reveal it to the world before I could if she has the chance."

"It's all quite fascinating, Frank, but I'm not a historian, a scientist, an archaeologist, or a reporter. How can I help? You don't need a crime fighter if there has been no crime!" the Phantom exclaimed in puzzlement.

"Oh, but there has been a crime!" Havens exclaimed. "Murder! A man in the Selma, Alabama area, disappeared in the same fashion as Williamson did eighty years to the day previously. But, this time we have a body. It was dumped in the middle of a muddy field and whoever did it left no tracks of any kind, just as there were no tracks left by whatever took him in the first place."

"Murder, eh?" the Phantom asked with interest. "Well, that is my specialty. But how do they know he was murdered and it wasn't a fall of some kind that killed him?"

"It was an open field with nothing to fall from for miles around. The body was covered with bite marks, at least on what there was left of him. He had been eaten down to the bone on most of his body. There was even a tooth stuck in one of the bones. Luckily, whoever did it left his fingertips and he was identified that way," Havens explained.

"Don't you mean whatever did that to him?" The Phantom asked as he raised one eyebrow quizzically.

"Dick, they were human bite marks," Havens said with a smile, not because he enjoyed knowing that detail, but because he knew it would make his friend spring into action.

The Phantom said nothing. Mentally, he was planning his route from New York City to Selma, Alabama so he could arrive there in the shortest possible time.

• • •

As a veteran combat pilot from the Great War, Richard Van Loan had no problem flying almost non-stop to his destination. The only delay was packing the various weapons and scientific apparatus into the various hidden compartments of his private plane. It would be Richard Curtis Van Loan, the famous playboy, that people would see arrive. The Phantom would only be seen when it was advantageous for him to allow that to happen.

When he arrived at the air field in Selma, he was amazed at how busy it was. The number of planes arriving would give New York City at Christmas time a run for its money. But the weather was a long way from New York at Christmas time. The air was hot and humid. Men sweated even though it did nothing to alleviate the heat. They were hot and worn out, and none of them showed any sign of being there voluntarily.

"Reporters," Van Loan deduced as he whispered to himself. If Havens was to get a scoop out of this now, it would be because the Phantom was the first to solve the mystery, not the first to arrive.

"Mr. Van Loan! Mr. Van Loan!" a slightly familiar voice yelled above the hubbub of the airfield. Van Loan turned and saw Jimmy Svenson, a junior reporter with Haven's *Clarion* newspaper. Officially, Van Loan was there in the capacity of Haven's representative, and Svenson's presence was intended to make that more believable. Svenson was a highly energetic and likable young man, and Havens was fine with providing someone to do the leg work for Van Loan while he did the real investigation as the Phantom. A small, slim red headed dynamo, Svenson fit the bill perfectly.

"Hello Jimmy," Van Loan said warmly. He had met the young reporter at several social functions. Most reporters treated such duties as a punishment, but Svenson treated each assignment as the one that would win him the Pulitzer Prize and make his reputation. "So what have you found out so far?"

"Not much," Jimmy admitted. "There are so many reporters here that it is impossible to be the first one to break a story."

Van Loan nodded his head. That was probably true for the bulk of investigators using traditional methods, but not the Phantom. Still, if the traditional channels were clogged for Svenson, he could still be of use.

"Then concentrate on the original story, Orion Williamson. Other newspapers are just printing summaries of their previous stories. I want you to look at all of the original documents you can, revisit old locations associated with it and reinvestigate everything you can. Check out the hoax of 1884, and find out everything you can about it too."

"It's a little late for Frank Havens to worry about getting to the truth of that, isn't it?" said a strong feminine voice from behind Van Loan. He turned around quickly and was confronted with a formidable woman in her late fifties. She was strongly built but with hardly an ounce of fat on her. She stood at least an inch taller than Van Loan despite being in flat soled shoes, and towered over Svenson, who stood barely over five feet tall. She was dressed in a heavy leather aviator's jacket, far warmer than anything worn by anyone else on the air field, but her skin was completely dry. She was such a strong willed individual that people around her got the impression that she simply refused to perspire.

"You're Amelia Johnson," Van loan said as he recognized his interrogator. "We met at a charity function two years ago in New York. I'm Richard Van Loan."

"No," Amelia Johnson said in a stern voice that showed by its tone that it was used to being obeyed, "what you are is not a reporter. Does Havens think so little of this case that he refuses to give it proper coverage?"

"You're not a reporter either, Miss Johnson," Van Loan said politely. "What are you doing here?"

"If you remembered anything about our meeting, Mr. Van Loan, you would remember that my ancestral home is in this area. I have homes all over the world, of course, but this remains my favorite. It is where I had my few happy childhood memories."

"Ah yes, I do remember," Van Loan said. Actually, he was merely playing the role of the bored playboy that the public thought that Richard Van Loan was. He vividly remembered being trapped by the gigantic woman in a corner of a charity gala while she tortured him at length with stories of her various real estate holdings and indicia of wealth. One memory stood out in particular.

"Would you happen to still have the exhibits that your father had in his private museum?"

"Of course!" Abigail Johnson said dismissively. "Among other things, we have the largest collection of Orion Williamson artifacts in the world, including the skeleton that was found in 1884."

"Then if you want the world to have a better opinion of your father, of course you will give my associate Mr. Svenson full access to it?" Van Loan said with a lazy smile.

• • •

Hours later, Van Loan was back in the air, but this time dressed as the Phantom. Svenson was enjoying what passed for Amelia Johnson's hospitality, but it was barely a passing grade. Svenson was left to his own devices in a warehouse with dozens of wood crates nailed shut. Amelia Johnson claimed that she had no idea which crate contained the skeleton, and it was up to Svenson to find it if he was intent on inspecting it. He had to pry open every crate and reseal it by nailing it shut himself. The crates were a foot taller than he was, and the pry bar that he had been given weighed almost as much as he did. Still, the little reporter was game and he believed that that he was seconds away from making the most important discovery of his life. In reality, Jimmy had already made the biggest discovery of his life but would never live long enough to know it.

In the meantime, the Phantom patrolled the skies. If there were no clues available to the latest disappearance on the ground, then the answer must be in the skies. If Homer Ludquist's body had been dumped in a muddy field without any tracks being left, then the body must have been dropped from the air. A cursory examination of the site by air suggested no new evidence. The Phantom looked at the sky above and thought he saw a dark shape move in a cloud bank above. He zoomed his plane closer to the clouds to investigate, and then found himself facing certain death as a giant zeppelin suddenly dropped from the cloud above him like a lead weight, headed directly for his plane!

The airship was closing in on him so quickly that there was no time to fly to either side, and it was too long to try to save himself by flying straight ahead. His only chance was to put his plane into a dive. The zeppelin was merely fall-

He had to pry open every crate...

ing under the influence of gravity, but he had the advantage, although few would call it that, of using his powerful engines to fly downwards at an angle. When he passed out of the shadow of the zeppelin, he desperately tried to pull the nose of the plane up. He managed to level the plane out and turn around before he hit the ground.

The zeppelin was exhibiting strange behavior. Its engines were obviously all dead, but it's rate of descent was decreasing. It soon began to hover a few feet off the ground, and after a few minutes, rocketed upwards again through the cloud banks and beyond.

"So that's how it's done!" the Phantom thought to himself grimly.

Returning to the airfield and his normal appearance, Van Loan began making telephone inquiries about missing zeppelins. None had been reported in the last month, so he made arrangements for older records to be examined.

Calling a taxi cab, Van Loan asked to be taken to the Johnson Estate. Although the cabbie knew exactly where it was, he was reluctant to go there.

"Look, mister," the cabbie pleaded. "You don't want to go out there. There's nothing there. Mrs. Johnson, she shut that place up years ago and swore to never come back. The only reason she done that now is the killings have started again."

"What do you mean killings?" Van Loan asked. "Only one body has been found."

"One found, yeah, but a dozen or more missing in the last month or so, maybe a few days less than that. They just haven't found the bodies yet."

Van Loan stroked his chin thoughtfully. Multiple deaths put a new spin on the case. And why would Amelia Johnson lie about the favored status of her Alabama home? He gave the driver a five dollar tip and his nerve suddenly returned, although he left at breakneck speed once Van Loan had gotten out of the car.

Walking to the front door of the main house, he was surprised to find the doors ajar. Glancing inside, he saw the prone body of Amelia Johnson lying on the floor. He approached her and her body suddenly moved, indicating life.

"Mr. Van Loan!" she cried. "We must check on Mr. Svenson in the warehouse! I left him there alone! There is a prowler loose on the grounds!"

She pointed the way to the warehouse and Dick sprinted there at record speed. The warehouse was filled with giant packing crates, all of them sealed. There was no sign of Jimmy.

"Whoever attacked me must have attacked Mr. Svenson as well and kidnapped him! I only hope that he is still alive."

Returning to the main house, Amelia summoned the police by the recently reconnected telephone, and when they arrived, Dick listened to the story that the woman told the police. It seemed that she had left Jimmy alone and returned to the main house. Hearing a knock at the front doors, she had opened them slightly to see who was outside, and was then viciously struck from behind.

"How could they knock on the outside but already be inside the house?" Mrs. Johnson wondered aloud. Her family name still had enough clout among the locals that a senior detective answered the question for her.

"It's an old trick, Miss Johnson. The thief was already on the inside of the house and knocked on the inside of the door to lure you here. Then, he grabbed what he wanted and left."

"And what they wanted was Mr. Svenson, no doubt. Probably a reporter from a rival newspaper. Do you agree, Mr. Van Loan?" Amelia Johnson asked in a voice as sweet as her disposition would allow.

"It's possible, of course," Van Loan agreed, "but why would they attack you? The warehouse is hundreds of yards from here. The perpetrator could have made off with Svenson without you ever knowing."

"Probably the thief wanted to make sure that Miss Johnson wouldn't be reporting this to us any time soon," one of the detectives offered. The rest of the police agreed with him.

Van Loan nodded. He disagreed with the detective of course, but would keep the rest of his theories to himself for use as the Phantom!

Later that night, after donning his domino mask, the Phantom entered the warehouse. Supposedly, Miss Johnson had left Jimmy opening wooden crates to examine their contents, but they had all been sealed when he had first seen them. He knew that because Jimmy was supposed to seal each crate after he was done with it that he may have been attacked before he could pry another one open, but the Phantom found that to be highly coincidental. He began examining the crates which showed evidence of having been recently reopened. Most of them hadn't been touched since the day they were sealed, but four showed evidence of being recently nailed shut again. The top board of one crate had a row of fresh nails in it, but none of the other crates had new nails that high.

Jimmy Svenson would have been unable to reach that high, so it was most likely nailed shut by someone other than him.

The pry bar the Jimmy had been using was still nearby, so the Phantom began using it to open the suspect crate. It took a great deal of effort as extra nails had been used to reinforce the entry panel, which was upright. The Phantom strained. He was far stronger than a normal man his size, but whoever sealed the crate had not wanted it opened ever again. Mighty muscles tensed and the crate finally gave way. It was empty, except for the body of Jimmy Svenson and a hammer. The Phantom marvelled at the simplicity of the murder yet its near perfection. Having found the crate empty, Jimmy stepped inside it to inspect it closer, and was struck from behind. Judging from the blood spatter, he was then struck in the head repeatedly while he lay unconscious until he died. The bottom of the crate was thick wood covered by absorbent carpet, so no blood would have escaped. The crate was then resealed, and all of the evidence was safely contained within the crate, invisible to anyone looking at its sealed exterior. The entire murder scene could then be shipped off to a warehouse on the other side of the world, where it would puzzle some underpaid archaeologist in a hundred years.

Someone was behind the Phantom. The person was walking as quietly as possible, but their steps made an unusual clicking sound. He whirled around while still crouching in the crate, and saw a giant of a figure approaching, dressed entirely in black and holding the same pry bar that the Phantom had used to open the crate. The Phantom suddenly moved his body slightly ahead, as if he was going to lunge at his attacker, but it was only a movement designed to provoke his attacker. The black giant swung, and would have crushed the Phantom's skull, had it not been for his own closeness to the crate. As it was, the end of the pry bar embedded itself in the top of the crate, making it useless.

While the black giant struggled to remove the pry bar, the Phantom actually did lunge at his attacker. He tackled the black giant solidly in the midsection, knocking him on his back with the Phantom on top of him. The shock had made the giant loosen his grip on the pry bar, and it still stuck in the crate like Excalibur waiting for Arthur to pull it free.

The black giant was a heavily muscled man close to seven feet tall and dressed in a long floor length black coat that had its collar turned up. A thin black mask covered his entire face and was barely thick enough to obscure his features, along with a black hat. Identification by the Phantom would have been impossible, especially as the giant intended for the Phantom to be dead in short order.

The giant brought his long legs towards his chest, wedging them between himself and the Phantom. He then pushed his feet towards the Phantom with all of his strength. The Phantom felt stinging pain in both of his legs as the giant did so. At that moment, he also pushed the Phantom off with all of his strength. Combined with the pain in his legs, it was enough to get the Phantom to release his grip and be flung off of him. As the Phantom struggled to his feet, the giant leaped to his and retrieved a dagger from the interior of his coat. He swung the deadly weapon, not only connecting the point with the Phantom, but knocking the Phantom's head against the embedded pry bar by the sheer force of the impact with the Phantom's body. Satisfied that he had dealt a death blow, the black giant ran off, and quickly disappeared into the night.

The Phantom was not dead, but was stunned by the blow against the pry bar. The stab by the dagger had luckily collided with the tiny, jeweled platinum badge in the shape of a domino mask that he kept in his pocket as identification with all law enforcement officers across the country. But perhaps it was not entirely luck, as Fate herself had often intervened on behalf of the Phantom when it appeared that death was certain.

Regaining his senses quickly, the Phantom decided that pursuing the giant was futile in the dark. He therefore resumed his investigation. The box that he died in was one of the first ones that Jimmy had opened, as none of the others except three nearby crates showed signs of being tampered with. Therefore, he was killed close to the point where Amelia Johnson had left him. Assuming that he had therefore found nothing, why had Jimmy Svenson been marked for death if he knew nothing? The Phantom decided to return to town as fast as possible. Whatever motive the black giant had for killing the young reporter, he had accrued it before the Phantom arrived. As Jimmy had not mentioned learning anything of value, he had not even known the reason for his death as the black giant crushed his skull again and again.

Havens had told him what hotel he would be staying at in Selma, so he assumed that Svenson would be in an adjoining room, as it was Havens' habit to arrange for that when booking hotel rooms for his staff. The theory proved correct, and the Phantom was able to easily gain entry to Jimmy's room from his own. He found Jimmy's journal, where he recorded the findings he had made each day, transcribed from the notebook he carried with him.

Jimmy had spent the time before the Phantom arrived going over old newspaper reports of Orion Williamson and the fraud of 1884. Obviously he had not mentioned this as Van Loan told him that he did not want to pursue that angle. Still, the reporter's journal made a good summary for the Phantom, saving him valuable time. The fraud case, it turned out, dealt with the veracity of the reporter who claimed to find the skeleton. He had claimed to have found it at a certain time and date in a thickly wooded area not far from Williamson's original point of disappearance. It had been proven that this story was impossible, as the reporter was actually at a social function at the Johnson Estate at that time, and this had been verified by half a dozen witnesses. The reporter than feebly gave other possible dates for his discovery, and they were also proven to be lies. As Amelia's father had been insistent that the real skeleton of Williamson had been found, it was naturally assumed that he was behind his employee's fraud. Svenson had written in the margin of his notebook "What about the skeleton?"

Svenson had made an interesting point. All of the news coverage focused on the fact that the skeleton could not be Williamson due to the fraud scandal surrounding it. No effort was made to find out who the skeleton really was once the fraud scandal had broken out. Svenson had researched the point, and there were no unsolved missing persons in the area other than Williamson, and no suggestion that there had been any grave robbing in the vicinity. The one description of the skeleton Jimmy had found was simply that it looked old enough to be Williamson and the fraudsters had at least made some effort to find a skeleton that could have been Williamson.

The Phantom shook his head in disgust. To him, the lives of innocent people were sacred, and there was no reason to believe that the man that skeleton had once been was not innocent. But, once it had been suggested by the press to not be Williamson, all interest was lost in it. It had been given to Amelia's father with some sarcastic remarks by the local police chief that it was the Johnsons responsibility to dispose of the skeleton they had planted.

Nothing else of interest appeared in Jimmy's notes except one name and address. All of the witnesses in the original Williamson case were long dead, but the reporter embroiled in the fraud case was still alive and lived at a local address.

Dawn was rapidly approaching and the Phantom had no time to lose. Removing his domino mask, he began working on his appearance with the contents of his disguise kit. He reddened his hair and added freckles. The evidence of the last ten years of aging was erased. He now looked like an older version of Jimmy Svenson, perfect for his intended role of a concerned big brother looking for clues to his little brother's disappearance.

· · ·

The former reporter was less than sympathetic. Although the Phantom played his role perfectly, the old man did not care about helping with Jimmy Svenson's disappearance as he had never had any intention of helping Jimmy Svenson. Yes, he was the reporter in question, and he had devoted his career up to that point to the Williamson case. He had learned everything there was to learn about the missing man through painstaking interviews with anyone that had ever dealt with him: family members, store clerks, doctors, dentists, former girlfriends, neighbors and acquaintances of all sorts. He had memorized the height, weight, and all other physical characteristics of Williamson before he died. If anyone was capable of identifying the skeleton as being Orion Williamson, it was him, and that was all he had to say on the matter. After the scandal, he had left journalism and made his living in advertising, where it did not matter if you had a reputation for not telling the truth.

The Phantom was about to leave when the old man made one last cryptic comment.

"Young man!" he yelled. "Everything I said about those bones was true! I can't swear to what other people said!"

The Phantom pondered these words as he walked back to his car. His thoughts were shattered by the sound of a gunshot. He ran back to the house to find the old man dead, with the figure of a giant dressed in black escaping in a car visible through a back window. Pursuit was impossible.

• • •

Going through the local archives, the Phantom, still disguised as Jimmy's fictional brother, had requested everything that Jimmy had. The only thing of interest was the record of who had made what disclosures about the skeleton. When asked about the discovery of the skeleton, the reporter had only announced the time and date of it. All disclosures about its location had come from Amelia's father.

Returning to his hotel, the Phantom found in Dick Van Loan's room several telegrams and phone messages that had been shoved under the door. They were the responses to his queries about missing zeppelins. One Swiss experimental ship that had left from Germany had disappeared in a transatlantic trip to America three months earlier. It was presumed lost at sea, although no evidence of that had ever been found.

• • •

The Phantom had returned to the sky. The mysterious airship had nothing to do with Orion Williamson or the fraud surrounding his skeleton, but it was undoubtedly involved in the death of Homer Ludquist and other local citizens. He found it again in a remote area with no habitation or air traffic, but following it was another matter. It was constantly changing its altitude as it cruised above heavy cloud cover, sometimes a thousand feet in the blink of an eye. As it changed altitude, so did the wind patterns that pushed the air ship along, as its propellers were long dormant.

The Phantom observed every detail of the zeppelin. All of the reports on it, although there were few, described it as an experimental model with an all Swiss crew. But, there was nothing unusual about its size, design or purpose that was evident. Its experimental nature must have to do with its internal workings.

The air ship plummeted, and the Phantom followed at a safe distance. It plunged through the clouds towards the ground in an almost vertical dive. As it approached a wooded area on the edge of a meadow, its descent slowed. Its back end started to rise, but its front end remained where it was. It was snagged! Cables of some sort were caught in the trees on the edge of the meadow.

The Phantom expertly brought his plane down for a quick landing. He then ran for all he was worth to the trees that had the zeppelin trapped. He climbed a tree that had one of the cables that held the air ship, and then started climbing the cable. It was at an angle, as the wind blew the zeppelin away from the trees, and he was able to lie down on the cable for stability, and pull himself upwards safely.

Then there was a loud snap! The tree that held the Phantom's cable broke under the strain of the zeppelin's great momentum, and the cable was now hanging straight down. The steel cable started to wear through his gloves as gravity now had a stronger pull on him. Hand over hand, he now pulled himself straight up. His gloves were thin and meant to give his hands dexterity while not leaving fingerprints, and not for protection. In seconds, the gloves would be shredded, followed by the skin of his very hands!

Suddenly, his progress seemed to quicken without any extra effort by his muscles. It was then that the Phantom guessed the horrible truth: he was being pulled upward from above by the murderous crew of the zeppelin!

Saving his strength for the inevitable battle, he only used his hands to not fall any further. He was quickly pulled onboard, and the onslaught of bony talons that tried to rip his skin from his bones convinced him that he was not among friends. He surged forward with all of his strength, catching them by surprise. Whatever his foes were, they were not experienced combatants. He was thus able to put some distance between himself and the hatch he had been pulled through. The Phantom then spun around quickly, and surged forward again, pushing several of his attackers through the open hatch into empty air. They did not scream or yell for help, seemingly oblivious of what was happening.

In the split second that occurred after he stopped his forward momentum towards the hatch, he saw some of his attackers in the light coming through the hatch. They were impossibly thin, looking more dead than alive. Their hair was long and filthy, their eyes bulging and lifeless. If they resembled anything at all, it was how zombies were depicted in horror films.

But that split second was all of the time that he had to observe the zeppelin's crew. They were upon him again, scratching, clawing and grasping. He broke free of their weak hands easily, but there was always more to take their place. Looking around him for a weapon, the Phantom saw a group of objects stored in niches on the wall of the air ship. Grasping one, he realized for the first time that they were human skulls, gnawed clean of any and all flesh. There were no other bones around, so they must have held some importance to the ghouls, but the Phantom could not have cared less about that at that moment in time. All he cared about was that they were the right size for throwing. He threw one at one of the men standing near the hatch. The impact knocked the zombie man out of the zeppelin, and then it itself ricocheted into the air and then fell down through the open hatch.

The loss of the skull suddenly became the main interest of the zombie men. Ignoring the Phantom, many of them voluntarily jumped through the hatch after the sacred skull. Grabbing another, the Phantom threw it directly through the hatch, and more zombie men jumped after it to retrieve it. By the time he had reached the last skull, his immediate vicinity was clear of zombie men, but he had no doubt there were more elsewhere in the giant ship.

Before proceeding any further, the Phantom pulled out his slim disguise kit. He had gotten a good look at one of the zombie men before he plunged to his death, and was able to easily recreate that ghastly image on his own face. The zombie men were mute except for low grunting sounds, which the Phantom, with his great mastery of mimicry, was able to easily imitate. The one thing he could not imitate was the corpse like thinness of the zombie men. Finding a blanket nearby, he covered his body from the neck down as much as possible and assumed the hunched posture favored by the strange creature and lurched forward to investigate.

The interior of the zeppelin was dark, so the Phantom groped along as best he could. He saw other zombie men, but only at a distance and illuminated by the light from windows. He was looking for either a normal human or evidence that they had once been on the ship. The further he went into the darkness, the fewer zombie men he encountered, so the Phantom assumed that if there were any normal humans onboard, the pitch black darkness of the deepest interior of the zeppelin was where he would find them.

As he shuffled further ahead in the darkness, he was suddenly attacked again. This time however, the foe struck the Phantom with a club of some kind in a concentrated effort and not the mindless actions of the zombie men. The Phantom assumed that this meant his attacker was still rational.

"Stop!" the Phantom whispered. "I am your friend!"

There was a pause in the blows, but they did not cease. Remembering the foreign origin of the ship, the Phantom tried the phrase again in French and German. It was the German version that made the blows from the club stop.

"Who are you?" the German asked. "I did not think that there were any other survivors."

The Phantom groped along in the dark as best he could.

"I am not part of the crew," the Phantom explained. "I am an American. I came onboard your ship to investigate."

The Phantom's words caused the German to laugh softly and briefly.

"No," the German replied. "You came onboard to die!"

Taking the Phantom by the hand, the German lead the Phantom through a maze of passages into a small room, and then barred the door.

"For once in my life, my curse has been a boon. I was born blind, so the darkness of the interior does not bother me. The crew members are afraid to come this far into the ship, so we are as safe as we can be. I think there are candles on the shelves in front of you. You may light one if you can."

The Phantom found a candle and lit it with a match from his pocket. He was in a supply room of some kind, and its door was barred from the inside by a makeshift steel bar that had been intended for some other use, but which served a far greater good now.

"I have all I need here to survive, but I have to use a nearby toilet on occasion, and I was returning from it when I encountered you. Who are you?" the German asked.

"I am called the Phantom," the Phantom explained.

"Ah!" the German explained. "I have heard of you. You are a brave man. I am sorry to have caused your death."

"You have done nothing to harm me," the Phantom said in surprise.

"Not directly," the German explained. "But I am Fritz Schmidt, the inventor of this death ship, and it kills everyone who encounters it!"

"Although I was born blind," the German continued, "I was a gifted chemist. I discovered a new strain of bacteria that emitted a buoyant gas when it died. I thought I had found the perfect gas for zeppelins. The length of air voyages could be extended almost indefinitely. The bacteria require little food, and reproduce quickly, and have a short life cycle. There was an infinite amount of the gas available at almost no cost! This ship is an ordinary zeppelin otherwise, but it may never touch the ground again!"

"But the bacteria cannot have an infinite food supply," the Phantom argued. "Eventually, the ship must crash."

"No Phantom," the German explained. "The bacteria do have an infinite food supply. They have learned to be cannibals, eating their own dead. They also absorb a portion of the gas emitted by their dead, and combine it with the air we breathe to create new food. They will never become extinct."

"But why does the ship behave so erratically" The Phantom asked.

"I did not examine the gas produced by the bacteria closely enough before my maiden voyage," the German explained ruefully. "It is not consistent in its quality. Some of the bacteria produce a variant that is a thousand times more buoyant than normal, and some produce a gas heavier than air. Plus, they do not behave uniformly to changes in temperature. It makes some of the bacteria produce huge amounts of gas that I did not predict in my sterile laboratory."

The German laughed again.

"I was a fool to ever leave it!" he exclaimed.

"But what happened to the crew men?" the Phantom asked.

"Another side effect of the bacteria," the German responded. "And one that I don't fully understand, I'm afraid. It is the one side effect that has no explanation. The entire crew, including myself, was exposed to the bacteria, and the entire crew except myself, have become mindless cannibals. When the ship drops low enough, they use ropes to either go down to the ground and grab people, or ensnare them and haul them up. I haven't seen that, of course, but I have been able to piece things together from what I have heard from their victims' screams."

"Could there have been as many as a dozen victims?" the Phantom asked.

The German gave a sad nod.

"I would be surprised if there were that few," he said.

"Why do they keep the skulls?" the Phantom asked.

"What do you mean? I have heard them eat the bones of their victims. They do not save anything."

"I found a bunch of skulls that had been set aside safely," The Phantom said. "They were so valued that the group of crew members I faced jumped off the ship to save them when I threw them out the open hatch. Could they have worshipped the skulls as some sort of idols?"

"That makes no sense," The German muttered. "They are all starving to death. They can afford to leave nothing behind of their victims, and they are not capable of thought, let alone starting a new religion. I have no idea."

"We must escape!" the Phantom exclaimed.

The German laughed harder and louder than he had since he had met the Phantom.

"I can't see you, friend Phantom, but I am sure that you do not have wings!"

"I am not an angel," the Phantom agreed. "But if you believe in them, you should ask for their help now. Let me lead you to the hatch I was pulled up. If we are lucky, it might still be free of crew men."

The Phantom and his ally moved as fast as they dared through the lightless hallways. The German's hearing was better developed than the Phantom's after a lifetime of blindness, and he was better able to determine if the path was safe with far greater accuracy than the Phantom. Eventually they reached the hatch safely.

"How high are we up?" the German asked.

"Not far," the Phantom said. "Perhaps five hundred feet or less."

"Not far?" the German asked sarcastically. "I take it that your wings have grown in?"

"This is the plan," the Phantom said, ignoring the sarcasm. "I have found the longest rope available. It is more than one hundred feet long. I have fashioned a loop at one end for my feet and tied the other end to a hook under the zeppelin that I was able to reach by leaning out of the hatch. You will ride on my back. Once the zeppelin is low enough, I will simply step out of the loop and take us both to safety."

"Simply?" the German asked without emotion. He was too shocked to be sarcastic. "I think our odds would be better of waiting for you to grow wings."

"I recognize the terrain we are drifting over," the Phantom explained. "If my theory is correct, we will both be safe in a few minutes."

"And if my theory is correct, you are completely insane!" the German exclaimed. "Still, I know of your reputation, Phantom. Let us hope that it is well deserved. Help me get on your back."

"Hold on as tight as you possibly can," the Phantom said once the German was in the piggy back position. "The first step will be quite spectacular."

The Phantom jumped out of the hatch. There was no way to lower himself and the German slowly, so this was the only option. He braced himself, but the jarring impact when the rope reached its end was enough to rattle the Phantom's teeth and make the German strangle the Phantom for a few seconds. Still, it was quickly apparent that they were still alive even though the Phantom was still wingless and did not need to change his name to the Angel Detective.

Within seconds, the airship had dropped so much that the Phantom's feet were only a yard or so from the ground. He freed himself from the rope and hit the ground running. The German must be in a state of shock, the Phantom reasoned, as his grip was getting tighter around the Phantom's neck. Once they were safely in a wooded area, the Phantom looked around to confirm their location. They were at the same spot where both Orion Williamson and Homer Ludquist had disappeared.

"You can let go now," the Phantom said to the German. "We are safe now."

The German only replied with a guttural sound that the Phantom recognized instantly. Grasping the German's arm, the Phantom bent over forward suddenly while violently pulling on the German's arm. The German was forced to release his grip on the Phantom as he was flipped over the Phantom's head and landed roughly on the ground. The German spun around to face the Phantom, and the Phantom was not surprised to see that the reason the German now sounded like a zombie man was because he was now a zombie man. There was no time to subdue the German safely. The Phantom pulled his automatic from inside his suit and fired, killing the German with a shot through his chest. He was about to abandon the corpse when he paused and used his pocket knife to sever the German's head from his body. Carrying the grotesque souvenir in a crude bag made from the German's clothes, the Phantom ran to where he had abandoned his car.

The Phantom drove back to the airfield and had the police summoned. They doubted his story until he showed them the tiny jeweled domino mask emblem he always carried with him to confirm his identity. This proved he was the Phantom, and to members of law enforcement everywhere, the Phantom's word was the truth. The police quickly gathered the scientists that the Phantom requested and gave them the German's head for analysis.

• • •

After agonizing hours of waiting, the Phantom received the report from the scientist with respect to their hurried work.

"This is truly amazing!" the head scientist exclaimed. "Dr. Schmidt did not discover a new type of bacteria, but a new form of protozoa previously unknown to man. Its chemical signature is unique and we were easily able to develop a test for its presence in the human body. You were correct Phantom, that the key to defeating the creatures is human brain tissue. A chemical in it is fatal to them if consumed. They can safely inhabit human brains, but once they have human brain tissue in their system, they die instantly and without releasing gas of any kind. They also require as much exposure to sunlight as possible to take over a host organism, which is how your German friend stayed unaffected for so long. Once they do take over an organism, however, the host takes on many of their characteristics, such as lack of intelligence and a preference for cannibalism."

"So they weren't worshipping the skulls," the Phantom said. "They were hoarding them because they instinctively knew that the brains inside the skulls could destroy them."

"Obviously," the scientist replied haughtily.

"Can you make a vaccine?" the Phantom asked.

"Yes, and very easily. Only a microscopic piece of brain tissue is required to cure a single man."

"Then I have no choice but to volunteer to be the guinea pig for both your new blood test and serum," the Phantom said grimly. "I have undoubtedly been exposed to the bacteria and need treatment as soon as possible."

The blood test was performed, confirming that the Phantom had been infected. They theorized that only his superb physical condition had saved him from becoming a zombie man, but that eventually it would have overcome him. The serum was injected into the Phantom's bloodstream, and worked almost instantaneously. A second blood test showed that his body was free of the deadly microbes.

"Quick!" the Phantom ordered the police. "Gather all of your men who are available! We must capture this deadly zeppelin! If we save the men onboard, we will save the world!"

A small army of policemen was gathered and dispatched to Homer Ludquist's farm under the command of the Phantom. They waited hours, but eventually the zeppelin came into view. Men grabbed the cables that dragged under the ship and secured them, trapping the ship near ground level. The police only had to wait seconds before the zombie men came scampering down the cables. The police appeared to be such a large supply of fresh meat that all of the occupants of the ship rushed towards them, not being able to realize that they were so badly outnumbered that they would never be able to overpower the police.

Instead, the police overpowered the zombie men quickly and subdued them. They were soon vaccinated by the police and whisked off for medical care for starvation.

"Good work Phantom!" the chief of police congratulated him. "You not only solved Homer Ludquist's murder, but cleared up more than a dozen missing person cases. Are you returning to New York?"

"No," said the Phantom with determination. "There are still two deaths to solve: the murder of Jimmy Svenson and the accidental death of Orion Williamson."

The Phantom left the Ludquist farm for the Johnson Estate. He would have to drive back into town and then to the Estate, which would take more than half an hour. Geographically, however, the site of the zombie capture/disappearance of Orion Williamson/death of Homer Ludquist was less than a mile from the Estate. Unknown to the Phantom, one of the policemen on hand who had overheard the Phantom's last words was a distant relative of Amelia Johnson and had been forced to promise to tell her of any progress made by the Phantom. He borrowed a horse from the Ludquist farm and was able to tell his third cousin, once removed, that the Phantom was on his way to the Estate less than ten minutes after the Phantom had departed the zeppelin.

The Phantom arrived to find the Johnson Estate on fire.

Most of the buildings were engulfed in flames, but the warehouse and main house showed signs of having been on fire the longest. He ran to the warehouse and looked for where it appeared that the fire had been started with an accelerant. It was a large stack of crates. He ran to the most inaccessible of them, a corner piece with crates above and beside it, and which could not be removed without starting an avalanche. Bringing a crowbar from his car, the Phantom began prying boards loose on the crate. His intent was not to open the crate but only make a hole big enough to reach in and grab some of its contents. The crates had been treated with chemicals to be flame retardant, so they were slow to burn, but they were not fire proof. The heat and smoke was unbearable, forcing the Phantom to run out as soon as his hand made contact with anything.

As soon as he reached fresh air, a hail of bullets forced him to seek sanctuary back inside the burning building. Holding his breath, he ran across the building and threw the object he had rescued from the burning crate through a closed window, and then jumped through the window after it. Picking up his precious relic, he circled around the building and cautiously peeked around the corner. He could not see the black giant yet, but the gunfire was a good indicator that he was there somewhere.

The Phantom looked at the sun with caution. The sun would be setting soon and the black giant would have the advantage of invisibility in the darkness, while the Phantom would be on unfamiliar ground in the dark. He had a flashlight with him, but to use it would turn him into a target. The black giant was not a great shot, but the Phantom did not wish to give him an opportunity for further practice.

The Phantom thought further for a minute. Forcing the black giant to shoot would have the advantage of showing the Phantom at least where his enemy was. He looked around the Estate grounds until he found a branch about six feet long and more than an inch in diameter. He tied his flashlight to one end of the stick but perpendicular to it. With practice, he was able to hold his flashlight out about five feet from his body in his left hand while he held his gun in his right hand. It was not a perfect disguise, but it would have to do under the circumstances. He circled around another building and walked into the open area of the Estate in the general direction from which the black giant's shots had come. The Phantom hoped that the black giant had not moved much and was just waiting for the Phantom to emerge again. But, this time he would not be silhouetted by light from the warehouse fire, and he hoped that would make all of the difference in the world.

His flashlight was on, and he pointed it at the edge of the woods. A shot rang out and the bullet kicked up dust from directly below the flashlight. The black giant's gun flash had given him away, and now the Phantom was able to return fire. The black giant fired another volley at the flashlight, and the Phantom did the same in return while turning his flashlight backwards to take away the black giant's target.

There was dead silence for ten seconds or more and the Phantom wondered if he had hit his enemy. He turned his flashlight forward again and moved its beam along the forest edge. There! He had found his foe and fired a shot directly at him.

The black giant's hat flew off and the Phantom knew that he had found his range. The black giant turned and ran into the forest. The Phantom turned off his flashlight and ran towards the black giant's last position. As the Phantom entered the forest, he found the black giant's hat. It was actually a hat sitting on top of another hat, sewn together so the brim would actually rest above the wearer's head.

"That answers that part of the puzzle," the Phantom said to himself. He cautiously entered the forest. His steps were miniscule as he did not want to step on any deadfall that would give away his position. After a few minutes, his right foot struck an object which moved slightly. He reached down and picked it up. It was leather and had a long prong at one end. He knew what it was in a second.

It was then that the black giant fell on the Phantom from above. The giant man must have climbed the tree in the hope that The Phantom would walk by. The impact knocked the Phantom down and backwards, and he struck his head on a fallen log as he hit the ground. Dazed but fighting for his life, the Phantom struck upwards with his left fist and all of his might. He connected with some part of the black giant, but he had no idea where on his body he hit. The black giant was similarly having trouble connecting with the Phantom, but a crazed blow did hit him directly in the face. Reaching upwards, the Phantom grabbed where the black giant's collar would be. Grasping it, he pulled the black giant's head forward, and heard it hit solidly on the same log that had dazed the Phantom seconds earlier, Knowing that he had a brief advantage, the Phantom grabbed his flashlight in his right hand and pushed the button to turn it on. The black giant was not only visible and close, but blinded by the light. The Phantom swung the flashlight upwards in a vicious uppercut, connecting with the black giant's jaw. The big man was stunned but still managed to land a kick with a bare foot solidly in The Phantom's chest. By the time the Phantom regained his feet and turned his flashlight on, the black giant had disappeared again.

The Phantom felt his way through the forest. It was heavily treed and would make gunfire next to useless. It also slowed the Phantom down and the few seconds in head start that the black giant had gained had proven to be very valuable. Suddenly, a mass of fury landed on the Phantom's head. Claws raked at his eyes. Cursing to himself, the Phantom grabbed his attacker and swung

The black giant fell on the Phantom from above.

him downwards, crushing the attacker's skull instantly. The Phantom turned on his flashlight to check the identity of his foe. The Phantom chuckled to himself. Although the raccoon he had just killed was a worthy foe, he doubted that it was behind the death of Jimmy Svenson. His search would have to go on.

A shot rang out and a bullet struck a tree in front of the Phantom. The black giant was nearby but the Phantom had seen no gun flash. He would have to find his foe and kill him in hand to hand combat. The black giant had proven to be a deadly enemy, and had killed a fine young man to simply protect a secret that was eighty years old. Such a ruthless killer would never allow himself to be taken alive. This was to be a fight to the death.

Suddenly the terrain became open and paved. The Phantom recalled seeing such a path way leading off from the courtyard of the Johnson Estate. The Phantom ran down the path towards the Estate as fast as a cheetah finalizing a kill.

The fire had spread and most of the buildings were engulfed in flames. The Phantom looked around the Estate grounds carefully. There was one small upwards jet of flame that was separated from the rest of the inferno. The Phantom made this his target and ran towards it. He had managed to still bring along the strange relic he had rescued from the warehouse fire. He wished to confront the black giant with it before he or the Phantom died.

The jet of flame proved to be the fire of a hot air balloon that was being captained by the black giant. With his enemy readying his craft for flight, the Phantom ignored all efforts at caution. He ran in the open and he ran straight at the balloon's basket. Just as the black giant released the balloon from its moorings, the Phantom leaped at him, and tackled him like a wrecking ball defiantly bringing down a giant building.

There was light now from the fire heating the balloon, but the mortal enemies were so entwined in grappling to the death that neither was able to use their gun. The black giant wrapped his hands around the Phantom's throat, choking him. The Phantom struck at the black giant's face, returning the blow he had received earlier. The black giant would not release his grip and if anything seemed to gain new strength from the hit. He knew that it was either him or the Phantom, and the desperation and insanity that had fuelled his rampage so far gave him even greater strength than before. The Phantom therefore concentrated on his opponent's arms, and delivered blows to the nerve endings in his enemy's elbows, followed by driving his thumbs into the armpits of the black giant's arms. The big man released his grip as his arms became temporarily useless, but drove his knee upwards into the Phantom's groin. The Phantom allowed himself to gasp with surprise but not feel pain. There would be time for that later if he won this struggle to the death.

"Talk to me you coward!" the Phantom snarled. "Why turn to murder!"

"Pride and honor," the black giant growled. "Things you would not understand."

"You killed a man from behind with a hammer. Are you proud of that? Do you find that honorable?" The Phantom said while grappling with the black giant. The Phantom was tempted to push the black giant as far as he could, pull his automatic, and fire at the balloon above. While grappling with his enemy, the Phantom had learned that the big man wore a bullet proof vest, but the balloon was now hundreds of feet above the ground, and the impact of the crash would undoubtedly kill both passengers. The Phantom had no fear of dying, and had always assumed that he would die on one of his missions, but he decided that now was not the time. He felt that he owed a duty to both Jimmy Svenson and Frank Havens to make the truth of these mysteries known.

With the giant's greater height, he had an advantage in leverage if not in strength against the Phantom, and the black giant was taking advantage of this. In any event, his strength was the equal or greater of the Phantom's, and the Phantom was impressed.

"Your strength is impressive," the Phantom grunted.

"I have travelled the world," the black giant boasted. "I have gathered herbs and magic powders from around the world. They dull my pain and give me great strength! I am invincible!"

The Phantom was not surprised by the answer. The black giant was both insane and a drug addict. He had faced such individuals before and they were always dangerous.

"And now," the black giant continued, "I will cross the border into Mexico undetected, and start a new life. And you, my dear Phantom, will start a new afterlife!"

The black giant had armed himself again with a short dagger. Undoubtedly his long coat held a small hidden arsenal. But, the coat could be a disadvantage as well as an advantage. The Phantom gathered up its excess material and impaled it on the dagger. To free it, the black giant had to use his other hand, meaning that both of his hands were in use. The Phantom rained blow after blow into the black giant's face. His face mask did not tear, but it was getting smeared with blood from the inside, obscuring his vision. The black giant finally freed his blade and began swinging it wildly. The balloon's basket was small enough that eventually the black giant would connect with the Phantom. The Phantom now had an opportunity to simply shoot the black giant at close range, and he decided that he had no option. He drew his automatic, and a blind swing of the dagger knocked the gun from his grasp and out of the balloon. The Phantom decided it was in his best interest to distract his foe for the time being.

"The death of Orion Williamson was eighty years ago," the Phantom argued. "Nobody can hold you responsible. The world would be grateful to know the truth!"

"I have already killed to keep that secret!" the black giant screamed. "And my family has killed others! If only the world had been satisfied when it was given the skeleton of Orion Williamson! The lost had been found! That should have been enough!"

"So that was the skeleton of Orion Williamson in the Estate's warehouse!" the Phantom yelled.

"Of course," the black giant cried. "It has been there since his death! His bones are still there and are now destroyed by fire!"

"Except his skull!" the Phantom said as he threw the skull of Orion Williamson directly into the black Giant's face. The blow stunned the giant but still did not knock him out. He swung again and again with the knife. The Phantom ducked the onslaught, but the giant connected with one of the ropes connecting the basket with the hot air balloon. Realizing what it was, the giant seized hold of it and began cutting it frantically, choosing suicide over defeat.

The Phantom attempted to leap onto the giant's back, but at that second the corner rope gave way, and the Phantom almost jumped out of the basket entirely. His knee collided with the giant's head, and the contact flipped the Phantom downwards so he could grab the edge of the basket. He was now hanging on the outside of it, but at least he was still in the air.

The giant was still blinded but knew his was around a balloon's basket by heart. He lunged to another corner and quickly cut its supporting rope without any interference. The basket now only had half of its original supports and was hanging from the remaining two ropes at a precarious angle. This made it easier for the Phantom to pull himself into the basket but harder for the black giant to continue with his suicide attempt. Using the edge of the basket as a handrail, he tried to pull himself upwards, but he could use only one hand as the other hand still held the dagger. Unable to find any footholds, he fell backwards and would have fallen to his death then if the Phantom had not made a desperate grab for the black giant's hand. Now the Phantom held onto the basket by one hand and held onto the thrashing giant with his other.

"Stop it!" the Phantom commanded. "It's all over now! Why do you want to die?"

"Like I said before, Phantom!" the black giant screamed. "There are things you don't understand, like pride and honor!"

The giant sank the point of his dagger as far as he could stab into the Phantom's wrist. Involuntarily, the Phantom's hand opened and released its grip on the black giant. The black giant fell hundreds of feet to his death. In minutes, the balloon hit a downdraft that was common in the area and the Phantom was able to safely drop to the ground. Racing back to the corpse of the black giant, he found that the giant had fallen on his own dagger, driving it to its hilt and killing him instantly. He rolled the body over on its back and removed its mask. He was looking into the face of Amelia Johnson.

• • •

"So the death of Orion Williamson was an accident?" Frank Havens asked. He was standing in his office at the *Clarion* and holding the skull of Orion Williamson. Dick Van Loan was sitting across the room from him enjoying a cigarette and glass of expensive brandy as best he could with a heavily bandaged wrist. The skull had been retrieved once the balloon had finally run out of hot air and landed.

"Very much so," Dick agreed. "According to records that I found, Amelia's grandfather, as well as her father, were avid balloonists. The grandfather was very much an amateur, and there are many local stories about his crash landings and getting caught in trees. The area has many sudden downdrafts, and the Williamson farm was close to the Johnson Estate. Undoubtedly the old man was out for a short flight when a downdraft brought him suddenly almost on top of Orion Williamson. Old Mr. Johnson avoided striking him, but some rope hanging from the balloon ensnared Mr. Williamson and carried him off into death and fame."

"But Mrs. Williamson said he disappeared into thin air!" Havens said in frustration. "And my grandfather believed her."

"Because that is what appeared to have happened," Dick explained. "All it would have taken was for her to look away for a few seconds, perhaps to watch her child, and her husband would be gone with no evidence left behind to say how or where. If she honestly believed that her husband vanished into thin air, why wouldn't people believe her?"

"But why did they conceal the death if it was an accident?" Havens asked.

"Well, Amelia at least confessed to that part," Dick replied. "Pride and honor. The Johnson family was very prominent at the time, and they did not want to lose their standing in the community. Therefore, they hid the body on their grounds. They knew that they were beyond reproach so that their Estate would never be a part of the massive manhunt that went on for Williamson. That body eventually turned into a skeleton. In 1884, that reporter really was at a social event at the Johnson home. He finally confessed as to exactly what happened after Amelia Johnson's death was revealed and he felt safe from retribution. She was the last of her line. He got tipsy and wandered off from the crowd, and ended up in the warehouse. He began looking through artifacts and found the skeleton. He had researched Williamson so thoroughly that he instantly recognized the skeleton as being his. He then returned to the party and announced that on that date at 2:20 p.m. that the skeleton of Orion Williamson had been found. He did not announce where he had found it because he was still there and thought it would be obvious. He presented the skeleton to the public, and the Johnson family thought this might be an opportunity to end public interest in the Williamson disappearance. They convinced the reporter, who was their employee, to give a false location. He never dreamed that they were involved in the Williamson death, but suspected they had come into possession of the skeleton by illegal means, and that was why they had not made it public themselves. In hindsight, he wouldn't have done so himself if he hadn't been drunk on free liquor."

"So how was it that Ludquist and Williamson happened to disappear exactly eighty years apart on exactly the same spot?"

"The date was a coincidence," Dick conceded. "But the location was almost inevitable. Wind patterns in the area have not changed in the last eighty years, and there is a prevailing wind with a downdraft which would take low flying airships over that spot time and time again. In a way, Ludquist was responsible for his own death, as he chose to stand in the exact same spot that Williamson had disappeared from."

"And the prevailing wind just blew that death ship over him, eh Dick?"

"Unfortunately so, Frank" Dick agreed.

"What happened to the poor wretches on the zeppelin, Dick?"

"Most of them are dead of malnutrition. A few will survive. They have no memory of what happened, but my blind friend Schmidt had kept a journal to pass the time. It serves as a record of what happened. All of the bacteria have been destroyed. Poor Schmidt. He was trying to help the world and ended up unleashing a monster."

"So what was it that first made you suspect Amelia Johnson?" Havens asked.

"Her ridiculous theory that Jimmy Svenson had been kidnapped," Dick replied. "She suggested that a rival newspaper did it. I liked Jimmy, Frank, I really did, but he was almost unknown in the newspaper world and those who did know him did not fear him. Besides, if anyone would have wanted to spirit him off, it would have been simplicity itself to simply haul him off into the nearby woods. Johnson was hundreds of yards away and it would have taken hours to discover that he was missing. There was no evidence of a struggle at the warehouse. Plus, there was no need for the kidnapper, if they existed, to attack Johnson. Lastly, there was no evidence that she had ever been struck hard enough to be knocked unconscious. She had no injury whatsoever. Plus when I finally laid hands on the giant, I found out that his mask was made from something I have touched too few times in my life, but I will never forget those times or how it felt."

"What was it Dick?"

"A woman's silk stocking," Dick said drily. "A woman might have some around but a man was unlikely to."

"But how did she pull off her black giant disguise? I've met Amelia Johnson, and she was formidable but not the juggernaut you described."

"Well, I told you about her trick hat. That added a few inches to her height. She was also wearing that traditional trick of women to appear taller: high heeled shoes. I wasn't able to see them when she wore them because of her long coat, but I could hear their unique sound. I also found one of them in the woods where she abandoned them so she could climb a tree. The added bulk was an illusion caused by the bullet proof vest she was wearing and the special padding her coat was lined with. It absorbed almost all of the impact of my blows, making her appear invulnerable. The drugs and her lunacy accounted for her strength."

Havens went silent for several minutes as he examined the skull again. Science had proven that it was in fact Orion Williamson's, and Havens' chain of newspapers had proclaimed the mystery was solved.

"Do you realize that there are still people who don't believe we know how Williamson disappeared?" Havens asked with a sigh. "They insist he was whisked off by magic or fairies or some such. I have spent my whole life trying to spread the truth, Dick. Why do I bother? There will always be those who do not believe it, and those like Johnson who will kill to conceal it."

"Yes," Dick agreed. "You will never convince the public one hundred per cent of anything. But, it's not your job to tell people what to think. It's your job to tell people all of the information available so they can make up their own minds."

"I still feel guilty about Jimmy Svenson, Dick. I really do. I sent him to his death."

"Your papers have painted him as a hero, Frank, and the man who solved the case. In a way, he was. Having known in Jimmy in life, I'm not convinced he would have not chosen certain death if it meant certain fame."

There was a pause in the conversation as Dick knew that Frank did not believe that for one second. Finally, Dick said "Gilbert Stevenson."

"Who is that?" Frank asked.

"A reporter. Family man. Works for a newspaper in Montgomery. Very well thought of."

"So?" Frank asked with a mystified look on his face.

"He had an appointment to interview Amelia Johnson the day after Jimmy was killed. It was cancelled by the police after the alleged attack on Amelia. I spoke to him, and he was following the same angle that Jimmy was. We saved Gilbert Stevenson's life, and probably several others. It doesn't justify Jimmy's death, Frank, but I think it justifies the work that we do, and that you are a big part of."

Frank poured himself a drink and sat down, still concerned but not as troubled. That was something he could believe in, and did with all of his heart.

THE END

WHY THIS STORY?

I own hundreds of books, and over my life I have owned thousands more, but one of the most beloved is LESTER DENT'S ZEPPELIN TALES. It is a collection of pulp stories by one of the all-time great pulp writers, and he shows how you can have a wide variety of themes on any subject including zeppelins. Naturally, I had to include zeppelins in this story.

Orion Williamson was a real disappearance case in Selma AB in 1854. At least that is what some people claim. A farmer walking across an open field disappears into thin air. The only logical explanation was zeppelins, but as they had not been invented in 1854, I settled for a hot air balloon. I love stories about missing persons, tribes and civilizations. It is strange to think that as more and more of the world is excavated or otherwise explored that they all haven't been found. Anyway, Orion was the basis for future legends about disappearing farmers as well as a short story by Ambrose Bierce, who later disappeared without a trace himself. If that's not proof of a major conspiracy by reptilian aliens, I'm not sure what is.

With respect to the choice of hero, the Phantom Detective was a natural. He was an expert pilot (actually he was an expert everything), and was therefore a natural for a story featuring zeppelins. He was also closely connected with a newspaper publisher, and it was newspapers that made the story of Orion Williamson famous.

The zombie aspect of the story was based on my own personal fears. Some people say that my fear of zombies falling on my head from the sky is irrational, but I think if the thought of that does not scare you, you are not very rational yourself.

The black giant aspect was based on those great Warner Brothers cartoons where the criminal was depicted all in black with a big black hat. In one Bugs Bunny special, he was revealed to be Porky Pig on stilts.

Amelia Johnson came from my desire to have a villain who did not want to conquer the world but instead had some personal motivation. Family pride, especially among those who consider themselves aristocrats in some way, is a dangerous motive in a class with lust and greed. Her name based on Amelia Earhart and the fact that she is a prick.

The bacteria element of the story was required when I realized that zeppelins just don't stay up in the air forever, and I had to come up with a way so that this one did. When in doubt, blame it on science. Isn't it amazing that we still don't have all of the scientific advancements that the Shadow and Doc Savage had in the 1930's?

The chase scene in the woods at night is from my childhood experiences playing a game called Purple Cow, which is a version of hide and seek played at night in heavily wooded areas, often without flashlights. What can I tell you? It was the 1970s and helicopter parenting hadn't been invented yet.

Poor Jimmy Svenson is based on Jimmy Olsen. Let's face it people. Even if Superman did have his back, the guy should be dead. Dead a thousand times over. Deal with it.

• • •

CARSON DEMMANS - is a freelance writer in Regina SK, Canada. Since 1994, he has been published more than 1500 times, with sales varying from a single sentence for cartoon gags to newspaper columns, magazine articles, and short stories. He is the author of four books so far, with more in the works. The first three are regional humor, but his most recent one is *OH MY GOD! THEY PRINTED THAT?*, a history/satire of sexist and racist comic books. If you like books about pop culture history, check it out on Amazon or at Bear Manor Media. He needs the money.

DOORWAY TO HELL
By Gene Moyers

The narrow street deep in an older Harlem neighborhood was dark. It was after midnight. The buildings that were still occupied were in darkness; their inhabitants asleep for hours. The few street lights still working were few and far between. A man stepped out from the shadow of the steps leading up to the boarded over front door of one five story, vacant tenement. He turned and crossed the street, casually swinging what appeared to be a bucket by its handle in one hand. He was thin and almost gaunt in appearance, dressed in worn clothing, wearing a long, ragged coat that hung to his knees. A flat cloth cap was pulled low down on his forehead

As he reached the opposite sidewalk, there was a crash of glass behind him. Stepping up onto the crumbling sidewalk he turned. On the top floor of the building he had just left, a window had blown out. Smoke billowed up and merged with the moonless sky while flames licked at the window sill. As he watched with a smile a second window blew out from the heat of the rapidly growing fire. A third and then a fourth followed almost immediately.

The entire fifth floor of the abandoned tenement was aflame. The man stepped back into the shadow of a doorway and watched intently as the flames rapidly spread, his eyes almost glazed with rapt attention. Smoke was pouring upward, obscuring what few stars were visible in the glare of the city lights. More windows blowing out disturbed the still night. A shout came from down the street. The thin man leaned out and looked left. Two doors down, a man awakened by the shattering glass was leaning out of a window. He was shouting, "Fire! Fire!"

This was music to the ears of the thin man. He smiled to himself hearing other voices now yelling into the night. He interpreted all the shouting and screams of horror as praise for his work. The sound of a siren came to his ears, growing louder by the second.

The man stiffened to attention as a fire truck, red lights flashing rounded a corner and screeched to a stop in front of the burning building. Uniformed firefighters spilled off the truck, pulling at hoses. The building was fully involved now. Flames were shooting from every window of the top three floors. While lower windows were now shattering from the heat. The street was now illuminated by dancing firelight but still a fireman atop the truck turned a spotlight on and played it over the front of the burning building.

More sirens could be heard in the distance. It was time to go. The thin man shifted the gallon can to his other hand and stepped out of the doorway.

Keeping his head down he turned to his right and brushed past a half-dressed man walking past, his head up, his gaze transfixed on the blaze across the street. The thin man walked past another building and turned into a narrow alley between two buildings and vanished in the darkness.

Another fire truck pulled up and more hoses were pulled onto the street. A crew was playing a powerful stream of water onto the front of the burning building. As the stream of water hit the flames clouds of steam billowed up mixing with the dark smoke. Many people, most with rapidly pulled on coats over their night clothes, crowded the sidewalks. Newly arrived police tried to push them back from the burning building to give the fireman more room to work. A red painted coupe pulled up and out stepped a man wearing a suit and a red fireman's helmet. He was most certainly a ranking officer of the fire department. He cast a critical eye over the scene before walking toward the first fire truck. Stepping over bulging fire hoses he looked about for someone in charge. He stopped dead in his tracks as his attention was drawn to the front of the burning building.

Caught in the glare of the truck's spotlight next to the concrete steps leading to the front door of the tenement, were hand painted red letters a foot and half high. The four letters read **HELL!** The paint was still fresh; drips ran down the side of the building from the roughly brushed letters. As the chief stared open mouthed at the word, the front door of the tenement above and to the left of the grim graffiti blew open and flames gushed out onto the stoop. Screams came from the horrified crowd.

• • •

Curtis Van Loan laid the newspaper down in his lap and picked up his drink. The morning edition of the *Clarion* had had initial news of the fire, but this evening's edition added details. Fire department authorities now were almost certain the fire was deliberately set. The only casualty had been an apparently homeless man sleeping in the basement. He was not a suspect since the fire had apparently started on the top floor. As Van sipped his martini his mind slipped easily into crime solving mode. Arson came immediately to mind. For profit? Revenge? He thought pointedly that this might be something for the Phantom to look into.

But not now. Glancing at this watch, he stood up and walked across his expansive living room. Entering his bedroom, he crossed to his dresser and picked out a set of gold cufflinks. He added them to the cuffs of his silk dress shirt. He then picked up his bow tie and stepped in front of a full-length mirror. He expertly tied the tie and critically adjusted his cumber bund. His reflection showed a trim, well-built young man; six feet tall with an athletic build that hinted at strength and stamina. Intelligent eyes stared back at him; a hint of a smile played about the handsome face. Satisfied, he slipped on his formal jacket and adjusted his cuffs.

Back in the luxuriously furnished living room, Van walked to the open doors leading to the red flagstone terrace of the penthouse he lived in. He closed and locked the French doors then headed for the front door of his penthouse and the hall closet. There he put on his dress gloves, top hat and picked up his walking stick. He ignored his overcoat as it looked to be another warm spring evening in the Big Apple.

Outside in the hall, he bypassed his private elevator and pressed the button to summon the express elevator to the lobby. It quickly arrived and Van stepped in smiling at the elevator operator, "Evening, Jimmy."

"Good evening, Mr. Van Loan. Big evening planned?"

"I'm meeting friends at the opera tonight."

Jimmy smiled back as he sent the elevator car downward, "I'm not much for that kind of high-brow stuff, myself. Geez, there's no beer, no popcorn. Where's the fun?"

Van laughed briefly, "Well, Jimmy, I'll grant you, opera is an acquired taste. I'll speak to the management about the beer and popcorn, though. It might make a pleasant change at the intermission." The two exchanged another laugh before the doors opened to the lobby. Van tipped a coin to Jimmy and strolled casually across the lobby. The uniformed doorman held the glass front door open for him and asked, "Cab, Mr. Van Loan?"

"Yes, that would be great, Frank."

Frank stepped to the curb, held up a hand and blew on his whistle. A yellow cab swerved out of the *Park Avenue* traffic and skidded to a stop at the curb. Frank held the door and saluted as Van got in and gave the cabbie an address. He nodded and the cab sped away.

• • •

Van relaxed back against the cushions of the taxi. It was nearly midnight. After the opera, Van and his friends had gone to an uptown club for drinks. Time had passed pleasantly with convivial conversation. A couple of people had asked about Muriel and Van had told them of her trip to visit family in Boston. Which reminded him he needed to give her a call soon. It had been a few days since they had spoken and Van missed her companionship.

Van was jerked from his musings by a siren growing louder by the second. His cabbie slowed and pulled the cab to the curb. Other traffic followed suit.

Seconds later a red painted coupe flew past going in the opposite direction, siren screaming and red lights flashing. Van frowned. He recognized a fire battalion chief's car. Must be a big fire somewhere. His instincts alerted, Van called out to his cabbie who was pulling out into traffic, "Turn around! Let's follow that fire chief!"

His cabbie pulled the unlit cigar from his face and glanced in the rear-view mirror, "It's kind of late to be chasing fire trucks, buddy."

Van leaned forward and passed over a ten-dollar bill, "I'm a lawyer and need the business! Now get going!"

"Whatever you say, pal!" The cabbie threw his left arm out the window, leaned on his horn and braked hard. Amid the screeching of brakes all around, he spun the wheel and cut in front of a big Packard sedan as he pulled a U-turn on the middle of the street. Ignoring the epithets and shaken fists thrown his way the cabbie straightened up in the opposite lane and pressed the accelerator down. The cab roared back northward, Van in the back hanging onto the strap mounted on the cab's wall above and behind the passenger door.

It wasn't long before they caught up with the chief's car. Cars were pulling over for the emergency vehicle and it was cleaving through traffic. Van told the cabbie to not get too close. If a cop saw them close on the tail of a fire vehicle, he might pull them over. Soon they were crossing 59th Street. Two blocks west Central Park split the city in two.

Minutes later, the chief's car skidded into a sharp right turn and headed east deep into the tenement slums. A student of crime history Van was well aware that this was the turf of several of the old neighborhood gangs of New York. While not the power they once were, it was still a depressed and violent area. A quick right a block past First Avenue and the fire was visible just ahead. The chief slowed but kept going toward the fire enveloping another five-story tenement. Van ordered his cab to the curb.

Hopping out, he paid off the cabbie and worked his way through throngs of people crowding the sidewalk to watch the horrible spectacle. A half block away he reached a police line and paused. He could have shown his famous platinum detective badge and would have been let through immediately but he was not in disguise and quite conspicuous in his evening clothes. He would be remembered and the Phantom took a great deal of trouble specifically to not be remembered.

Getting closer wouldn't have told him much anyway. He could see the building was finished. The firemen hosing the brick building down with multiple streams of water were fighting a losing battle. Soon the structure would be a hollow shell of unsafe brick walls. Even as he watched there came a rumble from the fire as some inner floor collapsed. Heavier smoke and dust billowed outward for a few moments then slowly dispersed across the street. Dust and ash rained gently down around and over the crowd like fine gray snowflakes.

Van could see multiple ambulances being loaded with injured people. Unlike the tenement fire he had been reading about only today, this building had been occupied. He grimly wondered what the "butcher's bill" would be. As his intelligent eyes scanned the scene his expression hardened. If this fire was connected to last night's, then the city might be in for real trouble. He decided it was definitely time for the Phantom to take a hand. Brushing ash from his shoulder, Van turned to leave but instead turned back and pushed through to a policeman who barred his way, "Sorry, no farther, buddy. Stay back!"

Van palmed his platinum badge his thumb covering the jeweled Domino mask at its center and spoke firmly, "Just a question, officer. Do they have any idea how this fire started?"

Seeing a detective's badge, the beat cop stiffened to attention and quickly replied, "Not sure at this time, sir. But I did hear one of the fire captains telling the sergeant that the way it spread so fast and hot he figured it must have been deliberately set."

"Thank you, officer." Van turned and thoughtfully made his way away from the fire. Pushing through curious bystanders he made plans to return to the scene tomorrow after the fire was out. There might be witnesses to question.

It did not take long to locate another taxi. Van gave his Park Avenue address and settled back in the cushions to think. Back at his apartment building he quickly crossed the lobby to the elevator and took it to the penthouse.

Once inside, behind locked doors Van quickly divested himself of his top hat, stick and gloves. Loosening his tie, he headed for his bedroom. The luxurious room was spotless. Van did not begin undressing; instead he stepped up to his large Empire style bed and pressed a concealed button on the wall behind it. A section of the wall silently opened where no trace of an entrance had been. Van quickly entered the hidden room, lights coming on automatically to illuminate the windowless space.

He had entered the hidden lair of the Phantom. Here was nearly everything he needed to fight the war on crime. Against one wall was a long bench on which were microscopes, a well-stocked chemical lab and other scientific crime fighting gear. Another wall held locked cabinets containing an arsenal of varied weapons of all types. Against the third wall there was a well-lit dressing table fronted by three mirrors. Nearby were racks of clothing of all descriptions from street clothing to uniforms, formal wear to bum's clothing.

Van walked to across to where a large scale map of the city hung on one wall. He reached out and ran a finger along eastside streets until he came to the location of tonight's fire. Plucking a colored straight pin from the wall he pushed it into the map. From memory he summoned up the address of last night's fire in Harlem. He pushed another pin into the map there. Stepping back, he gazed at the map and shook his head. Two buildings, both old tenements. One occupied and one not. Why these tenements in particular out of the thousands all over the city? They were both old but that could be said of most of the city's tenements. Many were as much thirty or forty years old. Who owned these two? Was it an arson-for-insurance scam? Or was it some crazed pyro who liked to watch fires? Van shook his head; not enough data. There would be much to do tomorrow.

• • •

The next morning Van put in a call to the *Clarion*. He was quickly connected to Miss Marsh, secretary to Frank Havens, editor of the newspaper, who quickly put him through to his old friend. Havens was a distinguished looking man, past middle age, keenly intelligent and a dedicated crusader against crime and injustice. In fact, it was Havens who had suggested to a bored Curtis Van Loan, that he try his hand at crime solving. Van had quickly solved a tough crime and brought in the criminal responsible. Finding a calling, Van had never looked back. He had eventually adopted the disguise of the Phantom to give him cover in his war on crime. Havens knew his true identity and did much to assist his crime fighting efforts. Many times, the Phantom Detective had been summoned by Havens either by a sudden phone call or by perhaps by the red signal light high atop the *Clarion* Building.

The familiar gruff voice came on the line, "This is Havens."

"Frank, it's Van. I thought I'd give you a call about some things I'm concerned about."

"Van, it's good that you called. I was just about to give you a call myself."

Van nodded as he said, "It wouldn't be about these fires breaking out around town, would it?"

"I'm afraid so. I've just been on the line to police headquarters with the chief of detectives. This is the third night running with out-of-control fires, all with this fiendish signature painted nearby. He's concerned that a psychopathic firebug is on the loose."

Van lifted an eyebrow at some of this new information, "Third fire? I missed any articles on the first fire. And, what's this about a signature?"

"The first fire was considered just an isolated incident. It didn't warrant much coverage. As for signatures, at all three fires there were words roughly painted on nearby walls, saying **Hell!** You can see why the police think a pyromaniac is on the loose."

Van replied, "Sounds possible. But you never know. It's time for me to take a hand in this game. But I need a favor, Frank."

"Whatever, you need."

"Okay, can you have Steve Huston check for any recent releases of troubled mental patients, especially any that may have had a history with starting fires."

"I'll get him right on it."

"Good. While he's at it, he might check on recent prison releases of arsonists. I'm going out to do some research myself. Can we meet for dinner later and compare notes?"

"Of, course. What about the *Publisher's Club*, say about eight o'clock?"

"That's good for me. I'll be there."

The two old friends then hung up. Van then walked to his bedroom. Opening the secret door, he entered his sanctum and took a seat at the make-up table. A past master at the art of disguise, he set to work. Quick work with make-up pencils under his eyes added apparent bags under them. Shadows along his jaw added length to it subtly changing his appearance. He used a color comb to brush artificial gray into his hairline at his temples and add a dusting of gray through the rest. Finished, the Phantom looked over his new appearance. He nodded satisfied that he now looked every bit the middle-aged reporter he would be playing today.

Next, he moved to his large selection of clothing. Carefully selecting an inexpensive but slightly wrinkled brown suit he changed into it and added a worn fedora to complete his look. Lastly, he moved over to a locked cabinet. Unlocking it he carefully selected a snub-nosed revolver and holster for it. These went onto his belt behind his hip, under his jacket.

On his way out the door, he put his platinum detective badge in his right-hand pocket and a pocket flash into his left. Ready to meet the world the Phantom left his apartment. Instead of making his way toward the express elevator, he turned the other way and walked to his private elevator. Exiting on the ground floor he turned away from the lobby and left the building through a private entrance.

A brisk walk of several blocks brought the Phantom to the garage where he kept his small fleet of private vehicles. Entering he gave Rogers, the garage owner the secret signal identifying his disguised self, reaching across to pull the lobe of his left ear with his right hand. Rogers nodded and went about his business. He was used to the odd comings and goings of the disguised man. He was well paid to keep the mystery man's vehicles serviced and ready for immediate use.

Choosing a non-descript Ford sedan, the Phantom was soon on his way. His first stop was downtown at the hall of Records. Inside he made his way to the city recorder's office. There posing as a reporter for the *Clarion* he asked for the legal ownership of three buildings he passed over on a list to the helpful clerk. These were the address of all three recent fires. The Phantom had received the third address from Havens during their conversation. With minutes the clerk returned with the sought-after information. The disguised detective thanked him and left.

Back in his sedan the Phantom looked over the list of owners. The three properties were owned by three different men; Jacob Forman, Alvin Prosser and Charles Benton. The Phantom was slightly disappointed. He had halfway expected them to be all owned by one person or company. This would have indicated a possible insurance fraud. If the buildings were unrelated, then fires set by a disturbed individual for the thrill were much more likely.

The Phantom's next step was the building burned in last night's fire. He made his way to the eastside. The street was closed off with temporary barriers so he parked a block away and made his way to the fire site. Although closed to traffic, pedestrians still came and went. Several were standing on the sidewalk staring at the ruins of the former tenement. It was only a shell. The floor was totally gone and the brick walls had partially collapsed. What was left was roped off with warning signs everywhere.

A man in a suit and wearing a red fireman's helmet was standing in front of the building making notes on a clip board. The Phantom pulled a small notebook from one jacket pocket and walked across the empty street toward what was obviously the fire investigator. Stepping up to him he spoke out confidently, "Gray, from the *Clarion*. Do you care to make a statement about the fire?"

The Fire Marshal looked up from his clip board, "Uh, sorry, we have no official cause for the blaze at this time. Our investigation is ongoing and we will release more information when our investigation is complete."

The disguised Phantom smiled in a friendly way, "Off the record, about how long will it take for you to decide on cause?"

The fireman shrugged, "Depends on the tests I've got to run. I've got some samples in my car." The Phantom pretended to make a note in his book, "What do you think that is?" He pointed to a scorched word painted in bright red paint on the side of the building about three feet off the ground. The word **Hell!** was scored and smoke stained but still legible.

The Fire Marshal pasted a neutral expression on his face and replied calmly, "I couldn't say."

The Phantom nodded, "I've heard that there were similar defacements at other recent fires in town."

The Fire Marshal put his clipboard under his arm, smiled and shook his head, "I wouldn't know anything about that." He turned and started across the street toward his official red coupe. As he passed the Phantom said, "It was arson, wasn't it?"

The Fire Marshal turned and gave him a sharp look, "Let's just say that I think my report will be fairly easy to write." He nodded and continued on to his car.

The Phantom waited until he had driven away before turning back toward the destroyed building. He slipped under a rope and approached the painted graffiti. Pulling out a pen knife he carefully scraped a sample of the paint onto his knife blade. This he placed in a small envelope he pulled from his jacket pocket. A minute later, he was back in his car and headed uptown.

Visiting the other two fire scenes, the Phantom took samples from the painted signs at both buildings. When he had all three paint samples, he headed his car north through the city. Sometime later as he neared the Bronx, the Phantom pulled over. Pulling a small case from the glove box, he proceeded to use this portable makeup kit to change his appearance. He subtly changed the lines on his face, added a gray beard and colored lenses to his eyes. Finally, he placed a pair of steel rimmed glasses on his face. He glanced in the rear-view mirror and the pleasant, rather owlish face of Dr. Paul Bendix smiled back at him. He replaced the kit and continued on through the Bronx.

Near where the Bronx became Westchester, he pulled up in front of a small warehouse. A "Closed" sign hung on the large overhead door. Getting out of his car, the Phantom used the stooped posture of Dr. Bendix to walk to the small side door. He opened it with a key on his ring and entered, locking the door behind him. Next to the door he reached out and flipped on three light switches.

Bright light flooded the large room. Instead of aging, dust covered machinery the light revealed rows of bookshelves filled with ledgers, books and journals of all kinds. Also revealed was a laboratory containing the most modern scientific equipment. There were tables of lab equipment and gear. An X-ray machine stood in one corner, a high temperature furnace in another. A full-sized spectrometer occupied space while a centrifuge sat next to it on a lab table. There was fully equipped darkroom and plenty of photographic equipment. In the back were rows of filing cabinets containing biographies of every important person in the country. Other files held information on crimes, criminals and any scrap of information that would assist the Phantom's crusade.

While his hidden lab at his Park Ave penthouse was well equipped for its size, this was where the Phantom went when he needed to work uninterrupted, in secret, doing the research that would help him solve whatever current crime confronted him.

This was where the Phantom went when he needed to work uninterrupted...

He immediately set to work. The three paint scrapings were separated and labeled. They were first examined under a high-powered microscope then they were each analyzed in the spectrometer. All three samples were identical to each other, confirming that they were probably painted by the same man. After analysis in the spectrometer, the Phantom looked at the results for a moment before moving to a shelf of reference books. Locating the one he wanted brought it back to the table. He opened the large book and began leafing through it. Finding the correct section, he quickly scanned it. Minutes later he had his result.

The Phantom frowned. The results were clear; the paint matched a red enamel paint used in the automotive industry. This wasn't something that you picked up in a hardware store. An item like this must be a special order. He pulled his earlobe thoughtfully, wondering how hard it would be to track down distributors of this kind of paint.

Locking up the warehouse the disguised detective left quietly in his car. On the drive south into Manhattan he had a lot to think about. Leaving his car at the garage; he re-entered his building through his private entrance and took the elevator to his penthouse. Changing out of his disguise he made a quick trip downstairs to check his mail. He was pleased to see a letter addressed in a woman's flowing writing. He lifted the letter to his nose and smelled the faint scent of a familiar fragrance.

Jimmy, the elevator operator, smiled knowingly at the Van, "Good news. Mr. Van Loan?"

"Just a letter from an old friend who's out of town." Jimmy nodded and winked.

Dumping the bills and advertisements on a side table. Van sat down and opened the letter. As he had suspected, it was from Muriel. He leaned back against the plush upholstery of the sofa to read the missive. Muriel was in Boston visiting old friends and would not be returning for another fortnight. She talked of her trip and activities and ended with telling him how much she missed him and looked forward to returning to the "Big Apple."

Muriel Havens was the beloved daughter of his old friend Frank. He had cared deeply for her for years. For her part she was very much in love with Van. He wished that they could be closer but he had to keep a certain distance from her. His secret war on crime had to be his first concern and he worried that she would be in danger if she knew his secret. She still got dragged in from time to time and as the Phantom he had had to save her from a dangerous situation more than once. This was annoying since he was certain that she was more than casually infatuated with his masked alter ego. Still the letter from Muriel put him in a good mood as he went to change for dinner.

Later that evening a taxi pulled up in front of the Publisher's Club located near Longacre Square. Inside the exclusive club, Van Loan was quickly recognized and shown to a quiet table where Frank Havens was already seated. He stood and the two old friends shook hands. After ordering drinks, they got down to business. Havens inquired quietly, "How's the investigation going?"

"As well as can be expected. I've visited all three crime scenes. They are most certainly the work of one man. His cryptic and ominous warnings signs are troubling and make a case for a mentally unstable psychopath. Especially, since I cannot connect the three properties by owners or location. Has Steve found out anything helpful?"

Havens replied, "I spoke to him this evening. He has checked every mental hospital and sanitarium in the metro area. None of them have recently released any patients with a history of arson."

Van sighed, "This arsonist must have a record somewhere! What about recent prison releases?"

"He was still working on it and will call you soon." Van nodded and the two men then ordered dinner. By the time they finished, they had agreed that there was nothing to do but wait for further developments.

• • •

Late that night, Van was rudely awoken by the ringing of his telephone. Jumping up he grabbed the receiver, glancing at his wrist watch. It was nearly three o'clock. It could only be bad news at this time of night, "Hello."

"Van? Frank Havens, here. There's been another fire."

Van asked, "Where?"

"Lower East side. 7th Ward south of Delancey Street."

"When?"

"It was reported about three hours ago."

"Anyone hurt?"

"Fortunately, it was an already condemned tenement. But it spread to neighboring tenements that had been converted mostly to sweat shops. We believe most everybody got out safely, but a lot of people are going to be out of work."

"Hmmnn… not much use going over there now. I'll go by tomorrow and see if it fits our pattern."

"That's the thing. It does. A witness saw someone painting on the building just as the fire broke out. He took off before police and firemen got there."

"That's great. Do we have a description?"

"The police have the witness downtown but our reporter got a statement. He couldn't identify the arsonist but he did say he was tall and very thin; dressed in rough clothing and of course he was carrying a can of paint and brush."

Van thought this over for a second, "Well, it's a start. What's the address?"

Havens passed on the address before hanging up. Van hung up the receiver and opened up the hidden room behind his bed. Inside he went to the map on the wall and pressed a red pin into it at the latest location. He frowned at the map. One more disaster to research. He wondered how many more there would be before he could stop the man behind them.

• • •

Late the next morning the Phantom, again wearing his reporter Gray disguise, visited the scene of the latest fire. This time was worse than before. Three tenements had been involved. The center one was totally destroyed. The brick walls had collapsed into a pile of smoking rubble. The two flanking buildings had caught fire as well. They were still standing but barely. The Phantom judged they were total losses and would have to be pulled down as well.

There were still a few firemen about hosing down hotspots and pushing debris from the street into piles. A man in a suit and fireman's helmet was making notes on a clipboard. This fire marshal was not the one he had talked to before so Gray walked boldly up to him, "I'm Gray from the *Clarion*. Have you determined the cause of this fire, yet?"

The Marshal turned and gave him an up and down look, "Not conclusively. We're still gathering information." He waved a hand at the burned buildings, "It's still too hot. It'll be days before we can get in there and make a firm conclusion as to the cause."

"But you do suspect arson; don't you?"

The man looked slightly annoyed. Before he could reply, Gray pointed at the base of the neighboring building, "Isn't that a sure sign that this was a deliberate act?"

"Maybe. We don't know who did that or when it was done.'

"Oh, c'mon! Wasn't a man seen running from the scene with a paint can?"

"Where'd you hear that?"

"There have been reports of eye witnesses."

The fire marshal looked sharply at the disguised Phantom. Finally, he tipped his helmet back slightly and took a step closer, "Look, pal. You didn't hear this from me and it's not going to be final for a while but, yeah this was arson." He waved a hand at the fire scorched painted words, "Whoever did this likes to watch and when we finally catch this guy, we'll find he's been setting fires since he was a kid." He nodded grimly, "He's on the record somewhere, crazy firebugs like this have long records."

Gray nodded and made a notation in his notebook, "Alright, this was all off the record. Thanks."

The marshal shrugged and turned back to his work. Gray turned and made his way back to his car. Inside he drove downtown to the hall of records. A half hour's research there gave him the building's owner and he was soon headed back to his apartment.

Inside his secret room, Van removed his disguise. He then moved over to his map of the city. Using a colored pin, he added the latest fire scene to the map. He then studied his list of owners and addresses. A study of the map told him little. The fires were wide spread, especially the latest fire on the lower east side. The buildings had three different owners. Last night's fire was interesting because it was the second fire at a site owned by one company. Was that significant? Van frowned.

Going to the city phone directory he looked up and wrote down the addresses of the three companies. He began making calls. He had business contacts all around the city. It took time and more than a few calls but he eventually had profiles on the three different companies who seemed to own most of the now burned properties. One was a commercial redevelopment firm. It bought older properties and rebuilt them or tore them down and built new structures. One was a property management company that owned and managed many properties in the city, including a lot of older tenements and warehouses. Another was a real estate trust that was moving into construction. It owned many properties but was having trouble with the city over code violations and required upgrades. That last company would bear closer scrutiny. An easy way of dealing with disagreements with the city would be to simply get rid of the building. Van went to bed with much on his mind.

• • •

Late the next morning, Van received a phone call on a private line in his secret room. Answering it, he was not surprised to hear the voice of Steve Huston, the *Clarion's* ace reporter and Haven's trouble shooter. The Phantom had worked with him before and trusted his work.

"Hello, Steve. Have you learned anything new?"

"Yes. I have some information you're going to want to hear."

"Good, what do you have?"

"A check with the State Parole Board shows that only two men with arson convictions have been released in the last few months. Uh, lemme see…"

Van waited while Huston consulted his notes, "Okay. The first is George Foster. He's apparently a paid arsonist. Done time twice for burning buildings for hire. He was released two months ago. He lives at…" Van wrote down the address Steve read to him.

"And the other guy?"

"His name is Fred Halquit. He was just released a couple weeks ago. There's no address on record, yet. But I do have his parole officer's name. He's a James Woodson and he works out of the city building downtown."

Writing quickly Van said, "Thanks, Steve. As usual you've really come through."

"Glad to help. Let me know if you need anything else."

After hanging up, Van entered his secret room. Taking a seat in front of his make-up mirror. He proceeded to put together a disguise he had used before. Careful work with added bags under his eyes and shadows along his jawline. Next, he combed a careful bit of gray thorough his brown hair. The effect was to give him look older and tired man. He smiled satisfied with his work. He then dressed in a worn, rumpled suit. He added a detective bureau badge to his belt and a regulation .38 revolver balancing it on his other hip. A worn brown fedora completed his look. He was confident he looked exactly like the part he was going to play.

Exiting the building through his private entrance, the Phantom picked up a sedan at his garage. He drove south and crossed the east River via the Brooklyn Bridge. Once in Brooklyn he located and drove past the address Huston had given him for George Foster. It was in a mixed neighborhood of small businesses and brownstone apartments.

He parked across the street and looked the building and street over. It was an average neighborhood with people coming and going. The building Foster lived in was occupied by a shoe repair place and a watch maker on the street level with two floors of apartments above. He noted the entrance to the upper floor for later reference and was about to drive on when a business down the block caught his eye.

Getting out of his car he strolled down the street until he was across from it. It was a garage. He lifted a foot onto a bus bench and retied his shoe while he quickly studied the business. A place like this might do body work as well as mechanical repairs. If so, it might have access to auto paint. Was it a coincidence that it was just down the street from a recently released arsonist? That was one of the questions he determined to ask Foster when he returned later that night.

Returning to his car, the Phantom re-crossed into Manhattan and drove downtown to the city building. Inside he asked around and was soon directed to a large office filled with desks and harried looking men behind them, typing up reports, talking into telephones or questioning other men. The Phantom didn't need to know that the men being interviewed were all paroled felons. They looked the part; hardened, tough looking men.

Asking, he was quickly directed to the desk of James Woodson. Woodson was a middle-aged man working in shirt sleeves, his jacket over the back of his chair. He had a receding hairline, a bit of a gut hanging over his belt and a cynical look on his face. As the Phantom walked up to his desk, he looked up suspiciously and said, "Yeah? What now?"

The Phantom flashed his detective bureau badge and said, "Detective Gray. I have some questions about one of your parolees."

Leaning back in his chair, a flash of interest flitted across Woodson's face, "Yeah? Which one's in trouble now?"

"Fred Halquit. He's only been out a couple of weeks. I heard he's assigned to you."

A sage nod, "Yeah, he is. Whatta ya wanna know?"

"First, I need his new address."

Woodson nodded and began stirring through the various piles of paper on his desk, "So, he's already in trouble, eh. I'm not surprised. He get caught setting fires again?"

The Phantom was taken aback at this statement but kept his calm demeanor in place, "Not yet. We're just rousting out anyone we know who might be doing these fires around town."

Woodson came up triumphantly with a piece of paper, "Ah, ha! I knew it was here somewhere!" He looked at the disguised detective and said, "I'm not surprised. When I read about the fires in the paper, I immediately thought of him."

"Yeah? Why?"

"Well, he's the only firebug I've got now." He frowned, "Might be only one any of us are working now," he waved a hand at the room. "And he's one sick firebug."

The Phantom pulled out a wooden chair across the desk from Woodson and sat down, "Huh! I'm listening."

Woodson handed the piece of paper across. While the Phantom wrote the address down in his notebook, Woodson leaned down, opened a lower drawer and sorted through some paperwork. He spoke over his shoulder as he did, "He's got a file an inch thick. First started setting fires as a kid. It's too bad that's juvie stuff. It doesn't count on his adult record otherwise he'd be in jail for life."

He came up with a thick file and dropped it on his desk. He opened it as the Phantom asked, "How old was he when this started?"

"He was ten when he was first arrested. Not enough evidence to put him in juvenile custody. But the investigators started looking into things and found lots of suspicious fires that just seemed to happen whenever he was around." He flipped through the file until he found the paper he wanted and lifted it up, "He was first convicted of setting fire to his high school. Did a year in juvie."

The Phantom questioned, "How about as an adult?"

"Several arrests. Lot of suspicions; but not enough evidence to prosecute. Only the one conviction; the one he was just released from. He did five years in Sing Sing."

"And the other arrests?"

Woodson shrugged, "Like I say; never enough evidence to go to trial. The guy is clever." He held up another sheet and frowned, "One time they had him but the chief witness disappeared. Case dismissed for lack of evidence."

The Phantom thought a moment before asking, "Has Halquit ever been evaluated by a psychologist?"

"Yep. I've got the report right here." He handed it across and The Phantom quickly skimmed through it. He did not like what he read. Halquit was more than troubled. The report was filled with words like 'pathological liar', 'paranoid', 'occasionally delusional.' The psychologist recommended he be remanded to a hospital for the criminally insane but was overruled. Instead Halquit got five years at hard labor. He did nearly four years before the parole board let him out.

Handing the file back, the Phantom asked, "So what are you doing about him?"

Shrugging, Woodson replied, "What I can. I've checked the job he's got. It's legit. I checked with the landlord and he's definitely living at the address he gave." He leaned back in his chair and sighed, "All I can do is keep an eye on him. Right now, he's coming in every week for an interview."

Interested the Phantom leaned forward, "Yeah? When's he due in next?"

Woodson flipped though his desk calendar. "He came in four days ago, He's due back Monday."

Gray stood up, "Thanks, you've been a big help. One last question; what does Halquit look like?"

"He's a thin drink of water. Almost gaunt. He's got dark brown hair going gray early." He thought for a moment before adding, "But the thing you remember is his eyes. They're empty. A lot of the time it looks like he's not there. Yah know what I mean? Like his mind is always somewhere else."

As the disguised detective turned to go Woodson added, "If you can pin these new fires on him and put him away, a lot of people will sleep better, detective."

The Phantom nodded, "I'll do my best."

Deciding that the afternoon was still young, the Phantom consulted his notebook and headed uptown. In midtown he parked and went into an office building. Consulting the lobby directory, he found that Benton & Associates was on the fourth floor. He took the elevator up and upon exiting the elevator quickly located the office he wanted. He was just reaching for the doorknob when the door was jerked open. A blonde woman was looking over her shoulder and speaking to someone unseen, "I've heard that line before. Mr. Benton can't hide from the press forever. I'm not the only reporter wanting to talk to him."

Before he could step back the blonde woman spun and crashed into him, the door closing behind her. She was a rather petite woman and she bounced off his chest, dropping her notebook. Surprised she opened her mouth to apologize but was beaten to it by the Phantom. Staying in character he said, "Take it easy, lady. Where's the fire?" This last was said with a smile playing across his face.

The rather flustered woman said, "I beg your pardon! I didn't see you standing there."

Picking up her notebook Gray handed it back to the attractive woman and a replied, "No. It was my fault." He held out his right hand saying, "Detective Gray, 10th precinct."

The woman took the hand and shook it with a firm grip, saying, "Delores Dixon. *New York Bulletin.*" A look of realization crossed her face, "Say! You're not here to question Benton, are you?"

Surprised by her boldness, he hesitated before replying, "Uh, I am here on official business, I'm afraid."

Dixie opened her mouth to say something else but instead smiled innocently, "Of, course. Let me help you." She turned and opened the office door wide gesturing for the disguised detective to enter. He did. The office was nicely furnished and the secretary an attractive young girl. Before she could ask his business, the Phantom spoke, "I'm here to see Scott Benton." The woman stood up and frowned, "I keep telling you reporters, Mr. Benton is not seeing anyone at this time."

Gray did not argue. Instead, he pulled his detective bureau badge off his belt and held it out, "NYPD. Detective Gray, on official business." The receptionist looked surprised. She hesitated, then said, "Wait here, please." She then turned and knocking once at an inner door, entered closing the door behind her.

She was back a minute later. She held open the inner door and said, "Mr. Benton will see you, now."

Gray nodded to her and walked past into the office. A dark-haired man with hair slicked back from a widow's peak sat behind a big desk. He was of

"NYPD. Detective Gray, on official business."

average build and middle age. His sharp eyes met Gray's boldly. Before Gray could speak, from behind him the receptionist squawked, "You can't go in—-" The slamming of the door cut her off. Looking behind him, Gray was not too surprised to see the reporter Dixon opening her notebook and pulling out a pencil. She gave him a dazzling smile.

Gray tuned back as Benton stood up and pointed a finger at Dixie, "I'll talk to the police but I ain't talking to no reporters!"

"Are you afraid of the truth, Mr. Benton?" This came from Dixie.

"Of course not! But I'll be da—-"

Gray held up a hand, "Mr. Benton, I don't think it's going to hurt anything if this reporter hears what I have to ask. You're not under suspicion. I just need to clarify a few things for our investigation."

Benton said nothing. Giving Dixie a glare that would have melted lead, he sat back down in his chair, "Ask your questions."

Gray sat in a chair across from him. Dixie remained standing near the door. "Alright, Mr. Benton, you own two of the recently burned buildings, do you not?"

"As I told those other detectives, yes I do. But only two of them. I don't know who owns the others."

"That's alright. We know. What I want to know is are the buildings insured? If so, for how much?"

Benton bristled, "Say! Are you trying to say I burned those buildings for the insurance?"

"I'm not saying anything, Mr. Benton. I'm just asking."

Benton looked suspicious for a moment, then straightening his jacket he said self-righteously, "Well, they're not! In fact, they're both scheduled for de-molition next month. You can check with the city. I've applied for permits to tear them down and rebuild."

Gray covered his surprise with a blank nod. This was not what he had ex-pected. He continued slowly. "So no insurance. I know you own many proper-ties. Are any other scheduled for demolition?"

"A couple. What's wrong with that? That's what I do. I build and renovate buildings."

'Hmmnn, do you know a George Foster or Fred Halquit?"

Gray watched for reactions as Benton answered, "No. Should I?"

"I guess not." Disappointed, the Phantom decided to retreat for now. He stood up, "Thank you Mr. Benton. That's all I have for now. I may be back though." Rising the Phantom turned and quickly left the office, Dixie trailing behind.

Out in the hallway, Gray replaced his fedora on his head as Dixie questioned him, "So, if you cops are thinking insurance; then you suspect arson. I knew those guys downtown were stone-walling! All that 'mad firebug' stuff was just a smoke screen. You got any hot suspects?"

Somewhat surprised by this reporter's persistence he replied, "I can't comment on an ongoing investigation. You should be aware of that Miss Dixon."

As they walked to the elevator, Dixie admitted with a smile, "Of course not. But occasionally, I catch one of you detective boys off balance." The Phantom smiled in spite of himself as they entered the elevator. In the lobby, they parted ways. Gray noted that Dixie immediately headed for a row of public telephones. He left the building and headed for his car.

• • •

Later that night the Phantom sat in his car on a darkened street across from the garage he had seen earlier. He was dressed in a dark suit. He wore a black Domino mask and his fedora was pulled down low on his head. In his pockets were his special platinum shield identifying him nationwide to law enforcement officers, his special master key and a small make-up kit. A .45 colt automatic hung from a shoulder holster under his left arm.

He was thinking over the conversations and information he had gathered that day. In addition to Benton, he had spoken to Jacob Forman and Alvin Prosser two other owners of the burned buildings. Forman was a landlord who owned many run-down properties. He had reluctantly admitted to having insurance but protested his innocence as well. Prosser had denied having insurance on his building and argued that he had been negotiating with the city to renovate it. Why would he harm that deal, he had asked? Both had denied knowing either Foster or Halquit.

The Phantom was torn. He still thought money might be motive for this series of horrendous crimes. But the possibility of someone as crazy and dangerous as Fred Halquit committing them could not be eliminated. Perhaps his next conversation would shed light on the subject.

Getting out of his car, the Phantom looked around. It was after ten o'clock and passersby were few. He crossed the street and walked down the street to the building where Foster lived. The street level door presented no problem. The Phantom had it open in less than a minute. Inside, mailboxes lined one wall of the tiny vestibule. He noted Foster's apartment number and headed boldly up to the stairs.

At Foster's door. He could see a dim light from underneath it. He knocked boldly and waited. There was a stir and a moment later a voice from the other side of it growled, "Who is it?"

The Phantom spoke in a low but authoritative voice. "Police. Open up Foster!" He quietly drew his .45 and tensed.

There was a pause before a lock turned, "This better be important flat—-" Using his shoulder, the Phantom threw himself against the door. The man behind it went sprawling onto the floor, uttering an oath as he hit the floor hard. The door flew open and banged against a wall. The Phantom caught it and kicked it shut behind him, his weapon pointed at the man on the floor.

The half-dressed man saw the masked man and gun, and went pale. He held up an empty hand and begged, "Don't shoot!"

"Are you George Foster?" the Phantom grated out.

A nod came from the man on the floor. He then whispered, "I know I was late but I'm up to date now! I swear! You can check if you want!"

The Phantom was confused, "What are you talking about?"

"Uh, you're one of Tommy's guys, aren't you?"

"No. I'm here to talk about the fires."

"What fires?" The man on the floor was now confused.

"Quit stalling, Foster. I know you've set fires for money before. Who's paying you now?"

Foster sat up. He cradled his right arm in his left and said, "You got it all wrong, man. I couldn't set any fires now if I wanted to."

His eyes now adjusted to the dim light; the Phantom could now see that Fosters right arm was in a cast from wrist to elbow. The white plaster now showing up in the little light from one lamp across the small walk-up apartment.

He leaned down to inspect the cast. It was not clean and white. It was dirty, with stains in a few places. He gestured with his pistol, "How long have you had that?"

"A couple of weeks or so."

"And how'd you get it?"

Unsure who he was dealing with now, Foster answered carefully. "Tommy 'Canolli.' I'm into him for some money. I got behind on the 'vig' and he sent a couple of his boys around to collect." He lifted his arm. "They gave me this!"

The Phantom nodded. He had heard of Tommy Vitroli. He was mobbed up with the 'organization.' He got his nickname from his love of pastry. He asked, "Where are you working?"

"Uh, I was dealin' cards for uh—, anyway I'm runnin' some numbers now until my arm heals."

And you're not working on any cars, are you?"

"Cars?' Naw, I ain't got one. I just got outta stir a while back."

Knowing he was off-track, the Phantom nodded to himself. He then leaned down and showed Foster the muzzle of his gun. "You were a torch in the past. You wouldn't be thinking of taking that career up again, would you?"

It was hard to tell in that light but he thought Foster went a bit pale. "No, no! I just did a long stretch for that. I don't wanna go back again."

"Good! Keep it that way." The Phantom reached behind him and opened the door. He backed through it and pulled it closed. He holstered his pistol and left quickly. Moments later he was in his car and driving away.

The address he had received from Woodson the parole officer was across town not far from Greenwich Village. He drove past the address to check it out. The building was an older brownstone converted to apartments by the look of it. The Phantom continued to the end of the block turned and parked on the side street. He got out, walked to the corner and looked the street over. It was after eleven o'clock and the street was deserted. Street lights lit the sidewalks but left pools of shadow. He walked casually down the street to the brownstone. His fedora and the darkness concealed his mask and to a casual passerby he would seem to be just a late-night renter returning home.

At the brownstone he confidently walked up the four steps and reached for the door. His body concealed him reaching into his pocket and pulling out his master key. The marvelous device, built for him by a master locksmith, was almost as good as a real key. Seconds later he was in the building's vestibule closing the street door behind him.

He didn't need to check the mail boxes. Woodson had given him the apartment number. The Phantom headed quietly up the stairs. As he climbed the stairs, he thought about the building he was in. It was certainly not an expensive apartment building by any means but neither was it a cheap tenement either. How could a recently released parolee afford to live here? It was one of several questions he soon expected to have answers to.

Reaching the fourth floor, he turned toward the rear apartment. Each floor had a front and rear apartment; eight total apartments. At 4R he hesitated. A light shown under the door. At this late hour? The Phantom drew his revolver and knocked on the door. Loud enough to be heard but not enough to wake the neighbors.

There was a rustling then silence. He knocked again, slightly harder this time. Firmly but not shouting he said, "Police. Open up!" There came a scraping noise and the squeak of wood on wood. Instantly the Phantom lifted his foot and smashed it into the door just above the door knob. The door flew open, smacking against the wall.

The living room he stepped into was dark. To his right an open archway showed a kitchen illuminated with overheard light. Ahead was a blank wall. To the left; the rear of the building, were two doors. One was closed the other open and dimly illuminated. The Phantom advanced toward this room. It was bedroom lit by a table lamp between the bed and rear window. In the open window a man was half through it. One foot and his torso were inside; the other leg and arm were outside the building.

The man was thin, wearing rough clothing. He was ducking his head through the window so his face was in shadow. As the Phantom lifted his automatic and yelled, "Stop!" he saw the gleam of glass in the man's hand just before he flipped it out toward the masked figure in the doorway.

The Phantom threw himself backward out of the room as the glass container hit the floor of the bedroom. It shattered and immediately the liquid it contained exploded into a pool of flames. Burning liquid splashed outward through the open door.

Rolling away from the flames the Phantom dropped his automatic and beat at flames on his lower pant leg and shoe with his gloved hands. His trousers smoking, he grabbed his pistol, lurched to his feet and ran out into the hall slamming the apartment door behind him. The small apartment was already filling with smoke. The door, its lock and knob shattered, did not close properly and smoke billowed into the hallway.

Holstering his weapon, the Phantom ran to the front apartment and pounded his fist on the door, yelling, "Fire!" repeatedly. Moments later the door was jerked open by a man in night clothes, a woman pulling on a robe was behind him. Reaching in the Phantom grabbed the man's arm and pulled him bodily into the hallway, yelling, "The stairs! Get out now!" He brushed past the startled half-awake man, grabbed the woman's arm hustled her into the smoke-filled hallway. He called out, "Hold your breath!" as he rushed her to the stairs. Her husband was halfway down to the next floor. There he urged the two downwards before plunging down the third-floor hall. A door opened as he passed. He pointed over his shoulder at the stairs and yelled, "Fire! Get out now!"

As he reached the rear apartment; the door was jerked open and a woman in her nightgown rushed out screaming. The Phantom did not hesitate. He grabbed her up and threw her over one shoulder. He then yelled into the apartment, "Fire!" Seeing no one he turned and sprinted toward the stairway Smoke was seeping through cracks in the ceiling and swirling down the stairway from above as he plunged down the stairs.

At the second floor landing he caught up and pushed through excited people in their night clothes. The woman on his shoulder was still yelling. He set her on her feet on the first floor, muttering, "Pardon me, ma'am," before turning and running down the hall toward the rear of the building. Down several steps, he reached the rear door, it was locked, He drew his .45 and put two lead slugs into the lock, jerked it open and leaped into the alley behind the brownstone his pistol up and leading.

The alley, normally in darkness, was now illuminated by dancing flames shooting from the windows above him. They cast moving shadows in the alley. His pistol scanned left and right. The shadows flickered tauntingly, as the flames waved and danced above him. Choosing left on a whim he ran down the alley. At the side street entrance, he stopped and looked left and right. He saw no one. He could hear shouts and screams from the street to his left and in the distance a siren, but the street in front of him was empty. Reluctantly he holstered his pistol. The arsonist had escaped.

The Phantom slipped his mask off and into a concealed pocket in his jacket. He then turned right and casually strolled away from the fire. He would circle the block and head back to his car when he was sure no one was taking an interest in him.

· · ·

Back in his apartment, Van changed clothes and showered. He threw away his burned trousers and found only superficial burns on his legs. He took care of these, thinking about what a near thing it had been. It was a miracle that no one seemed to have been killed when the arsonist made his escape. It also brought home to the detective the deranged madman his foe was. Using fire as a weapon in that enclosed space was insane.

Ready to face the world once more, Van called the private number of Havens. He wasn't surprised when the editor answered on the first ring. "Frank, it's me. I called to tell you there's been another fire."

He was not surprised to hear Havens answer, "I know. I got Steve Huston out of bed and he's down there now. I've talked to the chief of detectives and he's livid. Apparently, the police chief and the mayor are up in arms. The city is running scared and our story in the morning edition won't help any."

"I know. I was there tonight. I saw the arsonist. His name is Fred Halquit, recently released from prison."

Havens was nonplussed. "You were there! Are you alright?"

"I'm okay but it was a close thing. This Halquit is dangerous. Frank, I need Steve to do some checking for me."

"Anything you need. He should be calling in soon."

"Alright, I want him to check up on two men, Jacob Forman and Alvin Prosser. Find out anything you can about them. Businesses, funding, other buildings they own, anything that might help."

"Will do. What are you thinking? Are they suspects?"

"Maybe. Halquit is doing the fires. He's a psycho pyromaniac with a record that goes way back. But I still have a feeling that there's more to it than that."

"I'll get Steve on it, right away. Meanwhile what will you be doing?"

"I have an appointment very soon. In fact, I better get going, now." Van hung up and headed for his secret room. Quickly he changed his appearance to that of a thin faced, dark skinned man. He dressed in dark workman's clothes and equipped himself with all his usual tools of the trade. Leaving through his private entrance he was soon in his car headed back downtown.

A half hour later, he parked the car and walked the final block to his destination. It was an office building south of midtown. Ignoring the front entrance, the Phantom found the alley behind the building and slipped inside. Using his penlight sparingly, he located the loading dock and smaller back door near it. His marvelous master key made short work of the lock and he was soon inside the basement of the office building. He flashed the light on his watch. It was after four in the morning. He did not have much time. Soon, early maintenance workers would be arriving.

Elevators, including the freight elevator might draw attention from any security guards or all-night janitors so the Phantom located a stairwell and climbed upward. Minutes later he arrived at the seventh floor. Listening, at the open stairwell door, he heard nothing and proceeded on his search. Soon he was standing in front of a door. On the frosted upper half was painted Benton Development Corp.

His master key made quick work of the lock and a minute later the Phantom was inside. He re-locked the hall door and flashed his penlight around. He quickly located a row of file cabinets and began his search. He soon had files on each burned property that Benton owned in front of him. Benton had not lied. The buildings were all uninsured and scheduled for demolition in the next few weeks. Detailed demolition contracts to each building were attached. He raised an eyebrow as he read, these were interesting. He continued searching.

Soon he had found everything he was looking for. As he closed the last cabinet, he became aware of dim light beginning to seep into the office. A glance at his watch showed that it was after five am. Time to go.

Moments later he was in the hallway, the door re-locked behind him. The corridor was still empty but as he reached the stairwell door, he heard the elevator arrive on the floor behind him. He ducked quickly into the stairwell and clattered downward. In the basement he could hear distant voices but no one interfered as he let himself quietly out into the alley. Soon he was in his car headed home.

Back in his apartment, he showered and got a few hours of much needed sleep. He was awakened by the ringing of his private number. Answering it, he found Steve Huston on the line, "Hello, Steve. Have you got anything for me?"

"I do. When do you want to meet?"

"Uh, what time is it? Nearly noon. Hmmm, let's meet at the Green Spot. I'll be at the usual table at the back. Say, about 1:30."

"Right! 1:30. I'll be there."

"See you then." Van hung up the phone and began dressing for his meeting.

Later at the Green Spot, a popular gathering place near Longacre Square, Steve Huston pushed through the crowd looking for his man. Steve was a tall, enthusiastic young reporter. He had boundless energy and a strong nose for hot stories. He was excited to be working once again with the mysterious Phantom.

Steve scanned each table carefully. He had never actually seen the true appearance of the masked detective, as the Phantom always appeared in disguise. Then he saw it. To his left a thin faced, older man in a rumpled suit reached up and pulled on his left earlobe. That was the sign!

Steve changed course and at the table pulled out a chair and sat down opposite the Phantom. The detective set down his beer and waved for a waiter. He then smiled thinly at Huston and said, "Thanks for coming, Steve." The waiter arrived and the Phantom pointed at his beer and said, "The same for my friend." The waiter nodded and turned away.

The Phantom turned back to the "Ace" reporter, "So, what have you found out?"

Steve pulled a notebook from his jacket pocket and flipped it open. Reading from his notes he said, "Okay. Jacob Forman has been around awhile. He's been in real estate but has lately moved into property management; his own and others. He took a hit in the "Crash" and his business has never quite recovered. He seems legit. No shady deals. But, the word around is he's hurting for cash."

The Phantom nodded as he digested this. "And, what about Prosser?"

"Prosser's been big in real estate, too. He's now moving into construction. Re-building a lot of his properties and some new ones too."

"Hmmm, how's his finances?"

Steve shrugged, "Nothing unusual from what I hear. He's having a lot of problems with the city though."

"What kind of problems"

"Well, a lot of his older properties don't meet code and he's racking up a lot of violations, That's one of the reasons he's re-building so many of them. The city's giving him a lot of grief over permits."

"Building permits?"

"Yeah, and demolition permits too."

The Phantom took a thoughtful sip of his beer. He then smiled. "Thanks, Steve. That's helpful." He threw some money on the table and said, "Stay and enjoy your beer, I have to go."

He seemed ready to stand up, then stopped and asked, "Oh, I meant to ask. What did they say up at Sing Sing about Fred Halquit's parole?"

Steve waited until the waiter set down his beer and left before answering. "Uh, the warden was surprised that the board approved it. It wasn't what he expected."

The Phantom thought about that for a moment. "What do we know about the parole board?"

"Well, Halquit's board was three men. All long-time members, I guess. I don't have anything on them other than their names."

The Phantom raised an eyebrow at this news. "Really, anyone interesting?"

Steve shrugged, "Search me." He spun his notebook around and shoved it across the table. The Phantom picked it up. Seconds later he passed it back and smiled, "Thank you, Steve. That's a fine piece of work." He nodded once and disappeared in the crowd.

Steve looked at his notebook. What was so interesting? Just three names. What had the Phantom seen?

Back at his penthouse apartment, Van entered his secret sanctum and picked up the phone attached to a private, unlisted line. First, he called the city permit bureau. He inquired about building and demolition permits. Next the made several calls to various contractors he found in the city directory. Then made a long-distance call upstate. Finally, he made a call to Woodson the parole officer.

Van then gathered his notes and pored over them. A half hour later, he sat back and wiped a hand over his face. He then stood up and walked across the room to the large map of the city. He pulled pins out of the map, found a new location and pushed a red pin back in. Thoughtfully rubbing his chin, he murmured, "There."

* * *

Two nights later the Phantom prowled the second floor of an abandoned building in Brooklyn. It was a former shoe factory located near the East River, now closed for nearly ten years since not long after the crash of '29. Scheduled for demolition in a few weeks, it was unoccupied even by security guards or janitors. The structure was three stories tall, made of brick. Much of the first floor was open and two stories high. The metal machinery, conveyors and belts still crowded the work floor. Along one side of the main floor ran offices and two open stairways ran to the offices overlooking the floor. When in production the third floor had been for storage. From here long metal slides that ran down the back side of the building to loading docks.

This was the second night in a row that the Phantom had staked out this building. With the information he had gathered he was certain it was high on the list of buildings to be burned. More importantly it was owned by one of the men he had been investigating. The question was when? He just hoped other buildings weren't going up in flames while he waited here in Brooklyn.

He had put the previous night to good use and had scouted the entire former factory. He had initially thought there would not be much to burn in a brick building filled with machinery; but he had been wrong. Layers of leather dust covered everything and were silted up in every nook and cranny on the shop floor. There was also ten years of accumulated trash scattered everywhere; old newspapers, boxes, crumbling crates and piles of discarded leather scraps. Worse, the second and third floors were made of wood and many of the old offices were still filled with abandoned office furniture. It appeared that when the factory had closed for good, the owners had just walked away leaving plenty of flammable equipment and furnishings behind.

From the shadows of a second-floor office, The Phantom could look down on the shop floor through a window now missing its glass. The main floor was illuminated by tall, second floor windows on three sides. Despite this, the floor and machinery were in deep shadows. What little moon there was would not rise until nearly dawn. Having checked his watch minutes before the Phantom knew that was hours away. He hoped those hours would not be wasted.

Deciding it was time to make the rounds of the ground floor entrances once more, he turned and made his way into a nearly black hallway. Using his penlight shaded with a gloved hand he made his way to and down a set of stairs. Once on the main floor he drifted among the still and dusty machinery. He checked two doors, at the front and side of the building but saw no trace of entry. Earlier, he had pushed enough minor trash against every door to tell if it had been opened or not.

Threading his way past rusting machinery he made his way to the back of the building, then along a row of closed overhead loading doors to a single door in one back corner of the ground floor. Flashing his light for a second, the Phantom froze in place. Trash pushed against the bottom of the door had been pushed back in an arc. The door had been open since the Phantom's last check.

Still as a statue, the Phantom closed his eyes and strained to hear the smallest noise. All was silent. Moments passed. Nearly a minute later he heard the creak of a floor board somewhere above. Drawing an automatic pistol from

He had been wrong that there would not be much to burn...

under his jacket, the Phantom cocked it and glided through the darkness toward one of the stairways.

He did not chance a light. He had the advantage now and needed to surprise his quarry. He wanted to take the arsonist alive... if possible. Reaching one of the open metal stairways, he started up carefully. Metal did not squeak as old wooden treads would but the masked detective still climbed the stairs as silently as possible.

Reaching the second floor, he stopped once more to listen. No sound but his own breathing came to his ears. Then, moments later a low sound that sounded like the clink of glass on glass came to him. Glass? No one would be making any toasts here tonight. The Phantom drifted down the hallway, carefully watching where he placed his feet. At a half open door, he leaned in. Dim light from a dusty window showed the room empty except for a worn desk and broken-down sofa. He continued. Across the hall, an office overlooking the production floor was occupied only by more broken furniture.

Next came the office he had been keeping watch from. It too was occupied only by abandoned furniture. Moving silently down the hall he reached a slightly larger room near the front corner of the building. Perhaps it been a conference room at one time. He froze as he saw the dimmest of light coming from the open doorway. Easing toward the wall, the Phantom inched his way forward. When he reached the doorway, he leaned in just far enough to get one eye around the door jamb.

There was a large table with a broken leg pushed against the wall on the right. Several battered chairs were scattered across the floor. And, in the far corner a dark figure was crouched down with his back to the Phantom and the doorway. This bulky form shielded a small, flickering light placed low on the floor. Even silhouetted by the dim light, the Phantom could not make out much about the arsonist. His form seemed strangely lopsided. The Phantom could also see a cylindrical shape on the floor next to his left side.

The figure stood up slowly picking up a gallon can from the floor next to him. Once standing, the Phantom could see the thin figure was carrying a large bag slung from his right shoulder down across to his left hip. Upright he could be seen wearing a long overcoat and a floppy cap on his head. Between his legs the Phantom could see, in the corner, what appeared to be a candle on top of what of something that gleamed in the flickering light.

As he turned, a candle held in his right hand, the can hanging from his left, the Phantom stepped into the room. "Don't move Halquit! I've got a gun on you!"

Halquit was obviously quite startled. He jerked, almost dropping the candle, a hiss coming from his frozen figure. The Phantom reached for his penlight with his free hand as he stepped forward, "It's all over, Halquit! You've burned your last building."

The scarecrow like figure raised the candle. The Phantom could see his gaunt face twisted into a sneering laugh, "Ha, ha, ha, ha, ha!" In the middle of the laugh, Halquit blew out the candle and ducked as he dropped the can. The Phantom fired. The momentary flash from the muzzle of his automatic lit the room for a brief instant. His opponent had moved. He got his penlight out and flipped it on just as Halquit crashed a shoulder into him.

His penlight flew from his hand as he fell backward, hitting the floor hard enough to knock the wind out of him. The Phantom gasped for breath as he tried to bring his pistol to bear. Halquit cursed, as he grabbed the Phantom's gun hand, his free hand reaching for the Phantom's throat. He cursed fluently, his face so close that the detective could smell his breath and feel spittle hitting his face. Getting his left hand inside against Halquit's chest, the Phantom summoned his strength and heaved with all his strength. Halquit's gaunt form flew backward.

Both men scrambled to their feet. In the reflected light of his penlight that had rolled across the room, the Phantom snapped off a shot as the thin figure of Halquit dived through the doorway into the hall. He started after him with a snarl on his lips, then skidded to a halt after two steps. Spinning around he instead leaped for his penlight. Grabbing it up he strode to the corner of the room.

In the corner sat a half gallon glass jug. It was filled with a greenish, yellow liquid. The top of the jug was sealed over with melted wax. A small, very short candle was imbedded in this wax. A chill ran up the Phantom's spine. The candle had no more than a half inch to burn. Then it would begin to melt the wax seal and fall into whatever hellish mixture Halquit had filled the jug with.

Dropping to one knee, the Phantom leaned forward and carefully blew the candle out. He stood up and ran to the door way. There he could hear feet running across the floor above. As he ran toward the nearest stairway the Phantom knew what Halquit was carrying in his shoulder bag; another incendiary device.

Pounding up a set of stairs, the Phantom reached the open third floor in seconds. The beam of his light immediately caught the thin figure of Halquit across the room. The light reflected off glass near his feet. As the Phantom raised his gun, Halquit reached into his bag. The Phantom yelled out, "Halquit! You don't have to do this! You're being used as a patsy!"

Halquit's hand came out of the bag holding something. The Phantom took his pistol in a two-handed grip, along with the flash and called out, "Drop it, Halquit! Put your hands up! You don't need to do this!"

"And go back to jail? Never!"

"Don't make me shoot you. You don't want to die for somebody else who's just using you!"

Halquit laughed maniacally, "It doesn't matter, now! We're all going to die anyway!"

The Phantom could see Halquit clearly in the glare of his light. His eyes were wide and seemed to glitter with reddish light. The Phantom was sweating now. Halquit was clearly mad. There was no hope of taking him in peaceably. He struggled to find something calming to say. Taking a breath, he began, "Look Halquit, we can talk this out. Don't do anything ——"

At this moment, Halquit screamed out, "I'll see you in Hell!" His hand flashed forward as he laughed manically. The Phantom had only a spilt second to register a glass jar of some kind arcing across the room toward him. He squeezed the trigger and the big automatic bucked in his hand. He fired rapidly. Bam! Bam! Bam! His third shot shattered the glass bottle in mid-air. The instant the liquid inside contacted the outside air it burst into a cloud of flame. The Phantom frantically threw himself to one side. He hit the floor and rolled away from the growing lake of flames in the middle of the room.

Scrambling to his feet the Phantom shielded his face with one arm against the heat of the growing fire. He could not see Halquit but he could hear him, still laughing maniacally from somewhere on the other side of the room. Holstering his pistol, the Phantom scanned the room. The stairs he had come up were cut off. The fire was growing. He had only seconds. Then he saw it.

To his left was a low conveyor belt that ran around the perimeter of the third floor. In the glare of the fire, he could clearly see the unmoving conveyor ended at a square black hole that disappeared into a wall. It was the top of the winding metal chute that ended at the ground floor loading dock. With the heat of the growing fire hot on his back the Phantom sprinted to the chute and dove through the opening.

Scraping both shoulders on the edges of the opening, the Phantom found himself sliding face first down the metal chute. When in use it had been smooth and slippery. He couldn't see anything in the darkness but was surprised how fast he was moving. If the chute was rusty, it was not slowing him. Years of dust lubricated his passage and he spat out choking particles that billowed up in front of him.

The ride was only seconds but seemed longer before he tumbled head first out onto the concrete floor. He tucked into a ball as he hit and rolled across the floor. Pushing himself to his feet, he spat out dust and brushed at his clothes. The production floor was below the fire and relatively free of smoke. He could see the second-floor gallery aflame and pieces of burning material were even now falling down from the third floor high above. Spot fires were springing up across the main floor. Pulling his jacket lapel up across his face, the Phantom grabbed up his fedora from the dusty floor and ran across the dark, smoky floor. He was forced to dodge small fires that were now everywhere on the floor fed by the accumulated trash and leather dust. He was almost hit by a burning plank that fell next to him. He ducked and let it hit a milling machine he was next to, before continuing his run toward the back door.

Bursting through it into the alley behind the factory, the Phantom leaned forward, hands on knees and coughed for several seconds before he could draw in a clean breath. He staggered down the alley several yards before leaning against a neighboring building. The upper windows of the factory were spouting flames. Smoke billowed out of the open alley door. Shaking his head, the Phantom turned and trudged tiredly down the alley. Firemen and police would be here in minutes. It wouldn't do to be seen near the burning building; especially while wearing a mask.

• • •

A day and a half later, the Phantom pushed through the doors of the Pilgrim's Club located near Longacre Square. Approaching the maître de' he spoke confidently, "My name is Green. I've reserved a private room for 1 o'clock."

The maître de' replied, "Yes, sir. Right this way." As he led the way toward the rear of the main room he asked, "May I inquire as to how many people you are expecting?"

The Phantom held back a smile as he replied, "Just three. They should be arriving soon."

Arriving at a private dining room, the Phantom was ushered in. He took in the large table and chairs, Nodding, he said, "This will do nicely." As the maître de' began to leave, the Phantom added, "By the way, where are the restrooms located?"

"To the right, sir. Just before the kitchen."

"Thank you." After the helpful employee had left the Phantom moved quickly. He appeared today as a sharp-eyed man, with black hair and a neatly trimmed mustache. From within his jacket, he produced a black domino mask and quickly concealed his features. He then pulled on a pair of thin, flexible leather gloves. Lastly, he pulled a revolver from under his jacket, flipped open the cylinder, checked the load and held it in his hand. Taking up station against the wall behind where the door would open, he leaned back against the wall and waited.

After cleaning up the day before, Van Loan had made today's reservation. He had then sat down and typed up three cryptic notes. In a few words he had extended invitations that he was sure could not be ignored by men he wanted to see. They were picked up and delivered by private messenger. His guests should be arriving momentarily.

Moments later the there were voices in the corridor outside. The door opened and the Phantom stiffened. Two men entered arguing. One was saying, "Well, if you didn't; it must be Benton!"

As the second pushed the door shut behind him, the Phantom spoke, "Welcome, gentlemen. Have a seat. We'll get started shortly."

The two men spun around. Alarmed at the Phantom's presence and appearance both Prosser and Forman stepped back. "Who are you?" asked Forman

Prosser snarled, "If this is some kind of hold up, you won't get away with it!"

The Phantom lifted his revolver, "Don't be alarmed, gentlemen. I suggest you just sit down and wait quietly. All will be revealed soon." Forman looked doubtful but pulled out a chair. Prosser seemed about to argue but looking pointedly at the Phantom's weapon, he too complied.

Prosser cleared his throat, "Uh, I don't know what this is all about but—-"

He didn't get to finish because the door opened again and Charles Benton stepped through. The Phantom took a step forward and pushed the door closed with a bang. Benton jumped and spun around. The Phantom raised his gun and said, "Take a seat Mr. Benton."

"What is this?"

"Sit down next to your friends. We're going to have a little talk."

Benton, anger in his face turned and looked at the other two businessmen. Both Forman and Prosser shrugged. His face red, Benton reluctantly pulled out a chair and sat at the table.

Prosser spoke, "Who are you?"

"Just someone who's looking into all these recent fires."

That statement caused a thoughtful hush. Prosser looked surprised. Forman looked scared while Benton just went on looking hard at the Phantom. He finally asked, "Why are you wearing a mask? Who are you?"

The Phantom ignored him and continued, "You gentlemen may not have heard but the fires are now over. The arsonist behind them is dead."

This revelation caught all three men by surprise. Finally, Forman asked carefully, "Who was he?"

"His name was Halquit. He was a troubled arsonist with a long record."

Benton leaned forward slightly, "How did he die?"

"Why, he was burned to death in the fire that destroyed your abandoned shoe factory the night before last Mr. Benton."

Benton opened his mouth to say something then closed it abruptly. The Phantom looked over the men in front of him, "Burning buildings draws attention. So, it was very smart to bring in someone like Halquit. Someone with a history of fires and a record of psychological problems. Someone to point suspicion away from the real culprit."

"What do you mean?" this from Prosser.

At the same time Benton said, "I hope you don't suspect me. All the buildings I've lost have no insurance on them. There's no fraud on my part."

The Phantom turned to him, "No, you don't. But you are involved in demolishing and rebuilding those lots." He held up a hand as Benton started to speak, "And yes, I know you have legitimate permits for demolition. But I did some research and found out that professional demolition costs are quite high. It's a whole lot cheaper to bulldoze away burned wreckage than it is to demolish a building bit by bit."

At this revelation Benton went silent. His eyes narrowed. Forman said loudly, "So Benton's behind this!"

Benton shot Forman a dirty look. The Phantom turned and spoke to Forman, "Not necessarily. You Forman, have severe cash flow problems; and your buildings are insured. I'm sure you'll be able to put all that insurance money to good use." The triumphal smile fell off Forman's face.

The Phantom waved his gun casually toward Prosser, "And you, Prosser are having problems with the city; code violations and trouble with permits. Things are a lot simpler when those building have been turned into burnt rubble. All you have to do is have the debris bulldozed away. No permits, no inspections."

Prosser's face turned red. He swallowed and looked away. The Phantom continued, "I must congratulate you. Working together to spread out suspicion was brilliant. I don't suppose Halquit knew he was working for all three of you."

There was a brief hush before everyone began shouting. Benton stood up, saying, "I don't have to listen to this!"

Prosser shouted, "You can't prove anything!"

While Forman yelled out, "It's a lie!"

The Phantom laughed, "I don't have to prove anything. I just brought you here to let you know what I know. And what everyone else will soon know."

The Phantom backed toward the door saying. "I'll leave you gentleman to work on your stories, now. I hope they're good ones." Pulling the door open, the Phantom stepped into the hallway and closed it behind him. Turning he slipped down the hall and through the kitchen. His masked features caused a stir among the kitchen staff as he crossed through and exited into the alley.

Once outside the Phantom holstered his weapon and hustled toward the alley entrance. As he did, he removed his mask and stowed it away in his jacket. He also removed his false mustache to change his appearance. A moment later he emerged onto the side street, turned left and walked casually back toward the street on which the Club stood. At the corner he waited for the light to change so he could cross the intersection.

Glancing left he saw some kind of commotion in front of the Pilgrim's Club. A small crowd of people surrounded the entrance. They were shouting questions at three men exiting the club. Even from this distance he could recognize Benton, Forman and Prosser. He could also recognize the tall figure of Steve Huston and that slim female reporter; Miss Dixon. He had remembered her and she was one of several reporters he had made phone calls to earlier that day. He smiled as he crossed the street.

Once across, he could see Benton trying to get into an auto. He was being blocked by Dixon, while Steve Huston badgered the man with questions. In the distance the sound of sirens could be heard. The Phantom watched for another minute until the first prowl cars arrived, then turned away and walked to his own car parked down the street.

• • •

Later at his Bronx laboratory, in his Professor Bendix guise, the Phantom finished typing up a report. He found a place for it in one of a bank of file cabinets. When finished he called a familiar number.

At the other end, Havens answered, "Havens."

"It's me."

"I wondered when you'd call. I heard from Steve what went on this afternoon. He's writing up an article for this afternoon's edition."

The Phantom couldn't hold back a small smile, "I imagine the men involved will be getting a lot of publicity in the near future."

Havens asked, "How did you know all of them were involved?"

"I didn't; at first. There were only bits of circumstantial evidence that pointed to each one. And, there was that maniac Halquit with his paint brush. I knew he was the arsonist; I just didn't know why he was doing it. Then I started checking up on him. The building he was living in was owned by Forman. When I called Halquit's parole officer back he told me that he was supposed to be working for an auto repair shop. It turned out to be owned by Prosser. And Steve Huston had the final clue. Benton had a cousin with the same name on the parole board."

"Amazing! You took a chance trying to catch Halquit. You were lucky to survive that fire."

"Yes, it was a close call. But now it's over. I'm just filing away the report now."

"What's next?"

The Phantom smiled, "A good night's sleep. Then I'll wait for the next call."

Havens laughed, "You deserve it. But tomorrow, we're having dinner at the Publisher's Club."

"Are you buying?"

Havens answered, "I am. You deserve it."

"Then, I'll be there."

"Good. Tomorrow at seven o'clock."

The two old friends said their goodbyes and hung up. The Phantom closed up the lab, locking it securely before returning to his car. Inside he drove south toward home and some well-earned rest.

THE END

Couldn't Stay Away; The Phantom Revisited

A few years back Ron Fortier put out a call for stories for a new Phantom Detective anthology. I was surprised…not by the announcement but that it had taken so long to do it.

After all, the Phantom was one of the biggest names of the "Hero Pulp" era. His magazine ran twenty years; longer than either The Shadow or Doc Savage by a couple of years. A volume of his exploits would have to be a success.

I rushed to get a story into print, especially since I expected to have lots of competition for a place in the first anthology. I had a good story idea and I worked hard. In a couple of months, I turned it in with a sigh of achievement that I had made the first volume. I felt lucky to be included.

The book turned out great, although it took longer to get into print than I had expected. I was surprised it took so long to get sufficient writers interested. The book's artwork was impressive with great interior illustrations and a brilliant cover that is, in my opinion, one of the best pulp covers ever done by Airship 27. A pleasant surprise was that my story was nominated for a Pulp Factory Award. In fact, the book had several nominations and was very well received by more than a few in the New Pulp community.

Although my story did not win that year, I was still excited to be part of such a well-done book. So excited that I immediately began working on a new Phantom Detective story. I came up with a good idea and worked that into a detailed outline. It wasn't quite as inspired as my first Phantom story, but it was solid and I started in.

As I worked on this second story, something surprising happened. The buzz and interest about the first Phantom Detective volume quickly faded. Far more quickly than I thought it would. No writers came forward with more stories. Despite the quality of the book and response by reviewers there wasn't as much interest in the outstanding first volume as I thought there would be. I was disappointed. I thought interest would pick up but it really never did. Nobody climbs on a band wagon that's not moving, I guess. Eventually I lost interest as well. Tabling my outline, I moved on to other writing that was in demand. I still do not understand why Phantom Detective volume 1 wasn't a runaway hit. It's an excellent book and should have been.

Fast forward to 2020. Covid-19 came along and blew everybody's year into millions of pieces. My life was certainly changed. One of the biggest changes was my writing. You would think that stuck at home I would have all the time in the world to write. And this was true, unfortunately I had trouble getting motivated and my writing output severely slowed. Between the pandemic, forest fires and the never-ending election nightmare: somehow writing didn't seem all that important.

Finally, things began to stabilize this winter, and I decided to pull myself out of my writing slump. I went through my files and found lots of stories and outlines that needed to be completed. Among these was my long-forgotten outline for a second Phantom Detective story. I took a long look at it and decided it needed to be finished. So what if the first volume hadn't been the runaway success I had expected. My outline was sound and was well worth finishing. I dove in and within three weeks had completed *Doorway to Hell!*

The writing wasn't hard and went quickly. I was mostly happy with the story when it was finished but something was slightly off. All the scenes were there and the story was complete but the pacing wasn't quite what I wanted. I looked things over and decided that I did have all the scenes I needed but a few of them were just in the wrong place. Some tightening and a little shuffling of scenes and Voila!' Completed story.

Although not my favorite pulp character, I like the Phantom Detective. I found his adventures easy and fun to write. *Doorway to Hell!* might not net me another 'Best Short Story' nomination but it's a solid pulp detective story. Lots of disguise changes, multiple suspects and a big finale and reveal. What more can you expect from a Phantom Detective yarn. I am happy that this will kick off a new Phantom Detective volume. I hope you like it as well. And, who knows? Maybe we'll all be back here in the future for volume 3. See you then.

• • •

GENE MOYERS - studied European and Medieval history at the University of Oregon. He is also a U.S. Army veteran. He worked in the high-tech industry for some time and is also a licensed massage therapist.

An avid military gamer and role player, his favorite game was *Daredevils* a pulp based roleplaying game set in the 1930s. His love affair with the 1930s and pulps in particular stem from his first time reading a *Shadow* novel as a boy. Although interested in writing since a teen he did not turn to serious writing until 2000.

He is the co-author of *GURPS Crusades* published by Steve Jackson Games. He has written several stories for Airship 27 including stories published in all of the *Purple Scar volumes,* all of the *Domino Lady volumes, Mystery Men and Women vol.5, The Phantom Detective vol.1, Moon Man vol. 2, Dan*

Fowler vol.3 and *The Legends of New Pulp Fiction.* He has also written a story published in *Alternative Air Adventures* for Pro Se Publications and one published in *T.V Frost Scientific Detective* for Moonstone Books.

When not working on various new pulp projects, he is busy writing alternate history stories or horror adventures for his occult investigator, the *Dream Master.* Safe from Covid-19 in his hidden sanctum deep in the forests of the Great Northwest, Gene currently continues writing, carefully watched over by his wife and two lazy dogs.

THE MASTER YOUTHS OF JANUS

by Michael F. Housel

Richard Curtis Van Loan appreciated Muriel Havens' sparkling eyes, the way her fiery hair framed her porcelain skin and complemented her snug, black dress.

He had invited her to his Park Avenue penthouse under the pretext that she might type his scribbled frivolity: loose recollections of past adventures of crushed criminality that played more like fiction than fact, with changed names, locales and timeframes. The skewed content mattered little as long as the casual ploy worked.

"How soon do you need these?" She hoisted the overflowing folder. "There's a lot."

"No rush. Get to them when you can. It's not all that important anyway; just tall-tale anecdotes I felt compelled to jot down here and there. I'll compensate you for your time and effort, of course."

"I don't want any compensation. This will fill my free time, whatever there is of it. Maybe my father will even print the segments. Think of it—an ongoing, literary series by Wealthy, Renaissance Man Extraordinaire, Richard Curtis Van Loan. Wouldn't that be nice?"

"I like the sound of it, but I doubt your father would find such folly suitable for *the Clarion*. He's a hardnose publisher. He'd purge the comics if he could get away with it."

She smiled in a way that made his heart melt.

This prompted him to strut toward her, zigzagging past his many idiosyncratic objects (most of which were accessories for his crime-fighting alter ego) and watched her eyes grow dewy. In the process, she let the folder slip from her hands, its many sheets tumbling onto the lush carpet. Flustered, she bent down to retrieve them. He was about to tell her never mind, when from the window, a blinking, red light caught his eye.

It came from Clarion Tower: a signal from Muriel's father.

"Oh, hell," he murmured.

"I'm sorry, really I am. I'm such a butterfingers."

"Oh, no, I didn't mean you, dear. I, uh, just remembered I've something pressing to do." He sighed. "Never fails, don't you know?"

She stood with the papers clumped atop the folder. "I see." She cracked a hollow smile. "I know you're a busy man." She jostled the sheets into the folder.

"I don't think I messed things up too much. You did say the pages were numbered, right?"

"Yeah, most of them." He motioned her toward the door. "So, how about I call you tomorrow? We'll have dinner, hit a couple nightclubs. How's that strike you?"

"That would be nice, if you're not too busy, that is."

He reached over and opened the door, their bodies turning, their eyes meeting, hers glazed with woe and his with regret, but what could he do? He had no one to blame but himself for the lifestyle he had carved. Besides, if not for her father, he would have never gained the incentive to become the Phantom. He owed the man and as a further fortuitous result, even possessed a chunk of profitable stock in the paper. The arrangement was comfortable, ideal. All the same, there were times, and this was a major case in point, where he could not help but question his extracurricular pursuits.

"We'll see how it goes, Muriel." He kissed her brow. "Like I said, I'll call you." He looked down the stretch. "I'll walk you to the elevator, all right?"

"It's okay, Mr. Van Loan. I know the way."

He closed the door, listening to her heels click onward, and with that, she was gone.

He glanced back at the blinking light, its silent code loud and clear.

"All right already, Frank. I'm coming."

• • •

"Sure, this could have waited. I mean, there was no cause for you to get all decked out, but this has been bothering me for a while now. I figured why not flash the signal to chat before things got any stranger. Anyhow, you may have caught wind that there are these peculiar kids occupying the Brooklyn area, distributing books, or maybe one could call them pamphlets." Frank Havens grabbed one off his desk. "They resemble those of the Old West, the sort writers used to promote Doc Holliday and Johnny Ringo." He tossed it to Van. "Decent binding and quality stock. I'll give it that much."

Van adjusted his domino mask, which he had begun donning, along with his belted top coat and gray fedora, if only out of principled habit whenever Havens signaled. There was no telling if he might need to leap right into full Phantom mode after conversing, whether per rooftop meetings (where most of the exchanges commenced) or as in this case, in Havens' luxurious suite. Besides, it never hurt to get into character. The get-up ushered his investigative mood, and this would no doubt prove another warranted instance.

Van regarded the pale-pink publication, which sported an inky image of a flaxen-haired boy ascending within a smoky chamber, his eyes drawn big with wee sparks about his crown and arms outstretched in Christ-like emulation.

"*The Master Youths of Janus*," Van read aloud. "Now, there's a dandy title. Seems more suited to the funnies, wouldn't you say?"

"In a sense. It is adolescent dribble, no matter how you cut it, but with an odd undercurrent. As you may have noticed, it's penned by Anonymous. You ought to read Anonymous' work. Plays like Engle/Marx, but a lot edgier when one dips between the lines. It hints at what's been brewing in Germany, if you catch my drift."

Van flipped through the pages, his keen eye scanning various phrases: "The children shall lead...A master race to enlighten all ages...Young deities with the ability of flight...Powers so strong that the plebian sect cannot help but follow...A new sorcery for a new dawn to set all wrongs right."

"Does seem a trifle heavy. I take it these Master Youths of Janus are the good guys, like the Junior G-Men."

"Don't count on it. They're brazen, little bastards whether fictionalized or not. Yeah, they'll give you a book, but they'll also pick your pocket in the process with a load of persuasive talk. It's one of those deals where later down the line, you think about the hard-earned cash you shelled out for one of those silly editions and then kick yourself. A grocery cashier gave me that one—wondered why she had even bothered—and a few others have expressed their concern, calling in and writing to *the Clarion* in hopes of an expose. On the other hand, there are people—and allegedly a fair sum at that—who are exalting that crap, finding it all so exciting and what not. I overheard a fellow at the newsstand just yesterday suggesting it go the radio route or even be done up as a movie-serial."

"You want me—the Phantom—to check the intent. Sure, I can do that. I insist on it, in fact."

"Like I said, these tykes are all over the place, boys mainly, but there are a few girls in the mix. To get to the nitty-gritty, though, you'll have to alter your work schedule. They wander by day, in particular the mornings. Oh, and another thing—and it's a big thing in my estimation—a number of them have been spotted coming and going from the Raybel Institute. Goes to reason since it's right at Brooklyn's outskirts."

"Ah, Raybel. As I recall, your favorite institution of higher learning."

"It's sure as hell's no fair-to-midland NYU, Ithaca or Brooklyn College. I've good cause to despise it even beyond the suspicion that it's succored its accreditation through payoffs and syndicate links. The institute's founder, Joseph Hawthorne Raybel—may he rot in Hell—was a cultivated rabble-rouser, drumming up trouble with his batty agendas at every drop of the hat. If you were a bad guy in the post-Civil War era, Joseph Hawthorne Raybel was your faithful friend and ally. The institution is still tainted by the cretin's dirty dealings and anti-establishment babble, but parents send their kids there thinking it's a great source of progressive thinking. What a laugh. If those book-pushing kids are connected to Raybel's haughty intellectuals in any way, I'd love to reveal the fact to the extreme."

"Gotcha. Tell you what. Let me contemplate the matter some, sleep on it, and then I'll see what I can dig up. Deal?"

"Deal." Havers extended his hand. "As always, I appreciate your help."

Van shook with vigor. "And I'm always honored to grant it." He gave his mask a confident tug and then held up the book. "May I keep this?"

"By all means. Keeping it here just makes me feel dirty."

• • •

Van flopped into his comfy chair, robed and slippered, a cup of Earl Grey tea and ashtray-propped cigarette on the lamp table, his fireplace before him, dormant due to the warmer weather, though no less scenic for its aesthetic. With great scrutiny, he began to read.

The text's concept was, indeed, pulp-ish, featuring a band of intrepid youngsters who had been exposed to some strange, Mayan, mineral fumes, which increased their mental capacities to the point where they could read minds (or at least decipher a variety of behavior with heightened cunning) and float like cherubs about the air. In the fictional context, the minerals—offshoots of jade, flint, pyrite and cinnabar—were said to have been blessed by the Roman deity, Janus, one who could open doors, or in this instance thoughts, which allowed his benefactors to see the world from more than one "philanthropist" vantage.

The affected youngsters were led by a fair-haired adolescent named Henry Hunter, who convinced his peers to put their psychic prowess to the test against evil, though this evil seemed more a matter of age-old entrenchment: corporations, military factions and churches gone rogue, or had they? There seemed little to indicate that the given examples were any different than what existed in the real world.

"No wonder Frank Havens is upset," Van muttered. "A disguised intent for certain. And why are these kids distributing this stuff on the street? Why not make an arrangement with the newsstands and drugstores to sell their goods? Ah, but the personal touch of handouts is more persuasive to ensure those coerced donations."

He put the book down, finished his tea and cig, then closed his eyes. Tomorrow he would begin the investigation. Perhaps the matter would not be hard to unravel if he played his cards right. If these youngsters were as expressive as their text implied, communication (and consequential revelation) should be a snap.

• • •

The streets teemed of morning bustle. The sun was bright—too bright. As a night owl, Van was not used to such illumination. Nevertheless, there he was, moving among the people, looking both dapper yet inconspicuous enough within the industrious flow, his mask tucked within his trousers and his compact, makeup kit within his coat: ready to spring into action at a moment's notice.

"Hey, there, boss," a gruff voice called out. It was his Great War buddy, Jerry Lannigan. The beefy, rusty-crowned gent gave Van a wave as he finished gassing a faded Ford. "What brings you out in the sunshine, pal? You felt compelled to visit my new station? It's working like a charm, I'll have you know." He pointed up at the bolted, tin sign above the garage doors, which read in ornate, cursive scroll: LANNIGAN'S. "Can't deny it was a wise move, especially with the busy locale and having a few partners to back me. Given time, I might even hit your classy ranks, Mr. Entrepreneur."

"I've no doubt of that, Jer," Van replied. "For what it's worth, I've been meaning to visit, but to be honest I was just hitting the pavement on an investigative sojourn."

The customer paid Lannigan, who then walked over to Van with a mischievous glint. "Investigative sojourn, you say. I'd think you'd have taken one of your fancy autos for such a venture. More than anybody, you ought to know it's nice to travel in style."

"Oh, I parked the Duesenberg a ways down. Figured I'd handle this one by foot, mingle about, as it were." He paused for dramatic flair. "Looking for some kids."

"Ruffians?"

"These aren't the 'Dead End' sort." He pulled the book from his pocket. "They're more on the refined side."

Lannigan rolled his eyes. "I got one of those, too. Haven't had time to read the blasted thing, but I'll tell you this, the youngster who sold it to me—and mind you, he somehow wrestled me out of a stinkin' buck for it—was prim and proper in the weirdest way. You'd think he was selling magazines to work his way through college, but his pitch was more high-flown than that. From what I recall, he said he and his friends needed extra funds to push some sort of wacky campaign, but that folks would better understand once they read the content."

"You don't say."

"The kid I met looked like the one on the cover: sandy-haired, huge, spacey eyes, wide brow, vest and bowtie. There are others like him making the rounds, though not quite as off-kilter. All the same, you can't miss them. Something's off about them. Maybe you should implement your hobbyist techniques to see what they're really up to. I mean, you could become a regular Charlie Chan if you played your cards right, Dick Van Loan. " He grinned and winked. "Shoot, maybe you could even turn into another masked avenger, you know like that one *the Clarion* promotes."

Van cringed and chuckled at the same time, for though the Phantom employed Lannigan for clandestine ventures, his buddy had not made the connection the two were one and the same. For the sake of Lannigan's sanity and edgy temperament, it was for the better.

"Uh, thanks for the compliment, but all kidding aside, there's something quite confounding about this, something that keeps nagging me. For one, the peddled content isn't all that subversive on the surface, just escapist fun to the undiscerning reader." He opened the book, flipped to an excerpt and annunciated, "The mineral-churned fumes made Henry Hunter strong, sharp in the head and undaunted in spirit. He ascended, floating above the chemical spree and to his young confederates said, 'Rise with me. We will right all wrongs; help all those in peril with our newfound, scientific sorcery. From henceforth, we will be a genuine, crime-fighting league, known to good and bad alike as the Master Youths of Janus."

"Lovely," Lannigan remarked.

"Ah, but there's more, my friend." Van flipped to another page and continued, "The league surrounded the First National Bank. Henry Hunter swiveled as he rose off the ground and smirked at his friends. They were anxious to do the deed. They would sweep into the establishment and dazzle all who occupied it. From there, heroic Henry would sprint to the vault and with the assistance of his stalwart generals, Janie and Jimmy, round up the money bags and cart them away to distribute to those in need."

"Now that sounds more questionable than heroic, unless it's out of context."

"The extended context paints a more or less Robin Hood picture, but it's anything but. That's the problem, you see. How many will read this and get the hidden message? How many will mistake the unethical for ethical?"

"Yeah, I hear you." Lannigan paused and then with wide eyes pointed across the street. "And speaking of unethical, I see one of those kids now—right across the street—and by jingo, I think he's the one I met." Lannigan squinted. "Hell, I'm sure of it."

Van spotted a vested, bowtied, fair-haired youth stepping to the corner, a strapped stack of books tucked under his arm.

"Hmmm. Think I'll have a word with him. Excuse me, Jer."

Van cut his way through the traffic and approached the lad with carefree levity. The boy seemed content to remain stationed, as if he were sizing people up as they passed, considering to whom he should grant a copy.

"Hello, young man. What might you have there?"

The boy, who looked to be pushing thirteen, regarded Van with a scrutinizing glare, and Van reciprocated. He could not help but do so. The breadth of the boy's brow was noticeable, the side skin stretched in a peculiar way. His big, blue eyes twinkled with brilliance, and his nostrils twitched with an implied motivation. Without question, his facial composite was uncanny for its evolved implications.

Van pointed to the stack. "You have books there, eh?"

"Yes, books." The boy's tone was sharp. "What of it?"

"What of it? Well, I've been told you're giving copies away." Van cocked his thumb back at the garage. "The gentleman back there said you gave him one for a donation. He was rather impressed with the philosophical content and so suggested I come see you." Van pulled out his wallet. "In fact, I'd be happy to donate a sum for a several copies."

"You mean, that grease monkey read the text?" The boy giggled. "I am impressed. I had suspected he might be a wasteful prospect. I'm glad I didn't misjudge."

Van did not appreciate the youngster's insolence.

"Listen, young man, I'll have you know that fellow was a crackerjack sergeant-mechanic in the war—fixed planes like you wouldn't believe. He gave it his all on all counts, with plenty of gutsy derring-do to spare. I'd be a trifle more respectful, son."

"I do apologize." The boy swallowed his smirk. "It is our hope that people read the text—all people ultimately. What we present is more than mere adventure. If the, uh, war hero found value in the words, I'm grateful."

"All right, then," Van continued, pulling out some bills, "how about those copies? Let's say, three."

The boy's gaze then fell upon Van's pocket. "You already have one. Shouldn't that suffice?" The boy then glowered. "Did it come from the grease, um, the war hero?"

"What of it?" Van patted his pocket. "He simply wished to share your material, and I'd like to do the same. I can give them to others. That would help your cause, wouldn't it?"

The boy looked at him with stern incredulity.

"You're the boy on the cover, aren't you? Henry Hunter, right?"

"I should think that would be obvious, sir."

"Well, I'd like three additional copies, Henry Hunter, and if you wouldn't mind, maybe a little information."

The boy's stare grew swami-like. "I would rather not, to both requests."

"For heaven's sake, why not? I'm about to offer you a decent chunk of money and for a mere, few copies and like I said, some info. Not a bad deal."

"Perhaps per your perspective, but Professor Satana and Professor Tendrill have guided us on who should be the recipients at this stage. Though their advice sometimes leaves much to be desired, their overriding point has proven astute. As they have indicated, it is a matter of our applying instinct, gut feeling, that is, to candidates by studying their facial features. Faces are often shaped by the bearers' minds which often reflect an ulterior purpose. I sense from your features a conniving implication, precisely what we were told to deter."

Proven astute? What kind of thirteen year old street urchin spoke like that? Van Loan mused. *Totally not normal.*

"Professors, you say? Sounds more like a Fagin set-up to me. Nonetheless, these professors wouldn't happen to be affiliated with Raybel, would they?"

"Yes, Raybel and a number of other institutions throughout the nation and abroad, but Raybel at the moment. Professor Satana, in particular, is a highly regarded intellectual, and if you were an intellectual of even a small degree, you'd know his name and reputation well, but clearly you do not."

"Okay," Van growled. "Keep your books. Thank you." Van shook his head. "A real pleasure doing business with you, or make that not."

The youngster refocused on the street and its passersby, unstringing his bundle to swing a copy at a passing, plump lady. Van headed back to Lannigan.

"So, what did the little goof say? It didn't look like he gave you anything."

"He refused. This was much more difficult than I anticipated. A weird, little snoot, indeed."

"So what's the situation with him, with any of these kids?"

"I aim to find out." He winked. "Looks like I'll be paying Raybel Institute a visit."

Van then headed down the street, moving past more people, spotting more corner-bound children along the way, arms extended, propaganda distributed.

• • •

Van gazed into the mirror and adjusted the rubber strips about the bridge of his nose and under his eyes and then situated an uncouth, gray wig over his hair and glued on a matching beard. He capped the effect with a pair of thick, round specs and adapted a subtle slouch. Yeah, he looked like the stereotypical, absent-minded professor all right and wondered what that little snit would think now.

He tucked his makeup kit within his frumpy, frock coat and exited the men's room. He looked about the community center's welcoming hall, where a massive, painted portrait of its hairless, scowled founder hung and noticed across from it, among a fringing collection of fulsome, Picasso knockoffs, the indented names of faculty members housed within brassy frames.

DR. RUBEN SATANA...RM 3C

He looked above the name: ANTROPOLOGY DEPT: BROWNBRICK HALL.

So be it, he thought, and hobbled onward.

• • •

Van rapped hard upon the door and cleared his throat for added effect, trusting (though not expecting) the professor to be present.

No answer.

For good measure, he rapped several more times, when lo and behold, the knob turned. The door creaked open, followed by the protrusion of a flannel-sweatered arm.

Van backed up and hunched his shoulders to accentuate his aged effect. A man's face appeared, weathered from the sun, his widow-peaked mane, mustache and goatee a salty black. His eyes rolled up at Van, more languid than curious.

"Yes, how might I help you, sir?" His tone was soft though circumspect, his accent non-distinctive but seasoned.

Van smiled, while seizing the chance to glance inside: walls full of diplomas and honors, a standard, two-face Janus plaque and many shelves holding miniature replicas of Roman, Greek and Egyptian architecture, even several Jomon dogu figures and bridging them, photos of Aztec and Mayan pyramids. There were also books with stocky spines that cited ancient cultures, mythology and placebo-propelled psychology. Three in the latter vein stood out due to their blocky lettering: *Distortional Illusions Through Mineral Inhalation*; *Cerebral Evolution and You*; and *the Hidden Properties of Helium and Anti-Gravity: Discussions and Theories* The eclectic expanse reminded Van of his own extensive library, though his selections at least leaned more on varied practicality than eccentric supposition.

"I said, may I help you, sir?"

Van pulled the book from his pocket and declared in a guttural voice,

"Brilliant, absolutely brilliant." He waved the book before the man's face. "I only wish I had the words to praise it more, but the best I can conjure at this moment is—brilliant!"

A spark of enthusiasm entered the professor's eyes. "I'm glad you think so, sir, but tell me, how did you come to tie that item to me?"

"Well, one of your lads mentioned your name when I obtained a copy. It didn't take much to trace you here, and I thought I would toss caution to the wind and pay you an extempore visit. You are the man responsible, correct?"

"One of the lads, you say? How bold of him to share my name. Nevertheless, I am Professor Ruben Satana and yes, I am involved with the publication. I do appreciate the compliment. However, I have a heap of research papers to grade, and—"

"Oh, but please, Professor Santana, I only ask for a moment of your time. I am truly that enthused by the work you're influencing."

The professor hesitated. "I suppose I could spare a few minutes, but only a few." He looked down both sides of the hall. "Maybe it would be better if we took a stroll." He patted his chest and unleashed a raspy cough. "I could use a break and some fresh air, at that."

"But of course. That would be fine, more than fine."

The professor reached into his office and grabbed a cane. "Need a little assistance to get along. Didn't require this a few weeks ago, but got fairly stiff rather fast, all a matter of activities I've been indulging in with certain colleagues, but that's not here nor there." He laughed, but it sounded halfhearted. "We can walk in the courtyard. I do prefer the courtyard. I do like people around."

The poor man sounded feeble. How could he be a backer of such honed propaganda?

The professor closed the door and pointed his cane to the elevator. "We'll talk, just as you wish."

Van walked alongside him, noticing the man's awkward gait and wondered if he should have visited Professor Tindrell instead.

Van again placed the book before the professor's face. "So, did you write this?"

"No. The author remains anonymous."

"Yes, I got that much. Is this the only volume?"

"There's another. The youngsters now share the founding submission to get people interested. It's all done through a grant and lots of donations. Most of the youths have come from the orphanage and runaway center downtown, where the program was started. We're here to spruce the children up in the ways of academia. A few departments are involved."

"We can walk in the courtyard."

"All in alignment with the same philosophy, I see. The book certainly details it with clever precision. As I said, brilliant."

They entered the elevator. "I heard you, sir." The professor hit "1," prompting the door to close, and as they descended, he gave Van the onceover. "Are you a member of the faculty, someone new perhaps?"

"Afraid not."

"You look like a historian. Are you certain you're not affiliated with the Social Science Department? No, strike that. Perhaps our Communications sector? It also involves matters of historic reference in its own right."

The elevator halted. The doors wobbled open.

"Neither. Truly I'm not an employee here. I merely came to compliment you on your product, on what the children are sharing."

They entered the courtyard where a handful of students buzzed, some reading on benches and others having little, blanketed picnics, while a couple of white-haired men, groundskeepers, hunched about the shrubbery, trimming, and a bandana-crowned lady dug holes with a sharp shovel to plant transported flowers.

The professor paused and suckled the air, the sun dancing off his face. "Feels good, real good." He turned to the visitor. "So, you understand the text?"

Van nodded and gave a few approving blinks behind his phony lenses.

The professor waddled on, tapping his cane with playful vim. "All worthwhile thought comes through pleasant packaging. This children's literature illustrates that."

"I must agree. It's bracketed in a most affable and exciting way."

"In other words, it's sugarcoated. Tell me, sir, are you a fan of radical doctrine?"

"Only when I'm properly persuaded, as I am with the *Master Youths*."

He stopped and shot Van a stern stare. An inner face seemed to bleed through the weathered lines: a man with an ardent mission, of perhaps insidious purpose and plan. "Your name, sir?"

"Dr. Paul Bendix," Van proclaimed, pleased to rehash the label. "I'm retired, but remain an advocate of comprehensive science. I also hold a keen appreciation for cultural affairs. Anyway, my main hub, my lab, is stationed near the New York waterfront, but I'm now acting as a traveling scholar, you might say. At present, I'm making the rounds in dear ol' Brooklyn, in hopes of getting a handle on its intellectual and political flavor."

The professor nodded, his features softening a tinge as he recommenced his stroll. "I see. You've no doubt encountered the profuse patriotism in this myopic region. There's little budging of thought here, unless it's spiked with pizzazz. If our literary concept catches on, it could gain substantial backing.

Evidently, Baum did something similar with his fanciful, *Oz* fluff. What the *Janus League* offers, however, is more consequential. It can change things—change the world, if given the chance."

"And I should think all for the better then, Professor Satana."

"Yes, all for the better, Dr. Bendix. All for the great, illustrious good—a means to fix a world that is horribly flawed. And it will spring from right here, right at this very instit—"

Satana froze, then dropped his cane and touched his temple.

"What's wrong, Professor?" Van grabbed Satana and absorbed the twist of his trembling frame.

The professor looked at Van, his eyes bulging. The folks about the courtyard noticed what was transpiring and dashed over, as Van dragged the professor to a bench. That's when he saw the two children stepping forth: a brown-haired boy and red-haired girl, about Henry's age, the boy garbed similar to Henry and the girl in a simple, brown dress, their expressions stoic, their eyes blazing, though their features nowhere near as exaggerated.

"Let the professor be," the boy ordered.

"He doesn't need your help," the girl followed. "He's fine. It's just the result of a fleeting condition he has."

"Do tell," Van replied, as more people gathered round, including the grounds trio and a nervous looking lady who emerged from Brownbrick Hall, grasping a broom. Her dark complexion stood out among the pallid onlookers with a sincerity and pathos that Van found refreshing. "Sit down, Professor. Catch your breath. I trust someone will get help." He looked about at the gawking students, for a moment slipping out of character. "Where's the campus medical facility? Come now, just don't stand there—get someone here to help this man—a physician, a nurse. Now!"

From the side, Henry appeared, moving toward his friends, books depleted.

"He's better now," Henry proclaimed. "Look for yourself. He's fine, perfectly fine."

The lady with the broom looked at Van, her eyes wide and intense, her head shaking with doubt.

Satana unleashed another raspy cough, and then his expression grew placid, as if acting upon a hypnotic command. He smiled, his eyes remaining on the children.

"So, are you okay, Professor?" Van clapped to gain his attention. "Please Professor—you all right?"

"Yes, yes, I am," the professor replied with gusto and stood as if yanked by invisible strings. The students passed his cane onward, and Henry grabbed it, slipping it into the man's hand.

"Thank you, Henry, thank you."

The students began to disperse, along with the grounds crew, who gave one another tense shrugs, eyeing in particular the woman with the broom. Van then watched her turn, head bowed as she re-entered the building.

The children, however, lingered for a moment, looking unflinching and harsh. Santana regarded the three and explained, "This man—he's a good man. His name is Bendix, Dr. Bendix. He came to pay me, to pay us, a visit to compliment our work, our cause, and I—"

"We understand," Henry interrupted and turned to Van, studying the contours of his face and smiled in an insightful way, though a brush of sharp concern pierced through, strong enough to make Van cringe. "There's something distinctly familiar about you, sir, as if we may have met before, perhaps only a short while ago. And your eyes—that gray glint is unique—too much a coincidence to detect twice in one day." He focused beyond Van's messy crown and scraggy beard. "Yes, I do see the face beneath the face. The mighty Janus would be most impressed by the duality."

"By golly," Van replied with old-geezer zeal, "I dare say, you look familiar, too." He paused and snapped his fingers. "You're that famous cover boy, aren't you? The vigilant Henry Hunter. Am I not correct?"

The lad ignored the mocking acknowledgement and turned to his friends. "Though the Professor appears fine, it wouldn't hurt if I escorted him back to his office." He glanced at Van. "We appreciate your visit, sir, but I do believe it's overspent." He took the professor's hand, as the man jutted his cane to initiate a strut.

The brown-haired boy then regarded Van. "We'll be glad to escort you off campus."

"Either the front or back way will suffice," the red-headed girl suggested, "whichever you prefer."

"Oh, no, no," Van replied with a playful shrug. "I'd like to stay a spell if you don't mind. It's such a pretty campus, so many departments to investigate and from what I can gather, an impressive library, tiered of esoteric thought. Oh, I rather not pass up any of it, now that I'm here."

The children looked displeased, leaving Van to step back and watch Henry guide Satana back into the building.

Henry spoke to him in a haranguing way, uttering something about "risk of exposure" and a "need now to move fast," finger shaking and face tightened with urgency.

Someone tapped Van on the shoulder.

Van turned to regard a tall, hefty guard. "You're not allowed on campus without a pass."

Van smiled. "How might I obtain one, please?"

"You can't, unless you receive special invitation. I don't suppose you have a special invitation, do you?"

"Well, young man, I came to converse with Professor Satana, as perhaps you saw."

The guard looked to the side. Van followed his gaze and noticed Henry's friends giving him an adamant stare.

The guard turned back to Van, looking even meaner. "The professor didn't leave any word that he was expecting anyone. Don't know how you even slipped in, but no matter. It's time to skedaddle, mister." The guard waved Van onward. "Come on, now. Let's go."

Henry's friends walked into the building.

Van could have used some ju-jitsu on the big bloke, but what would that have proven? It was better to go along and head a few blocks down to where his Duesenburg was parked. He could find more information through other means. After all, the Raybel library was not the only source in town.

• • •

"You'll stay in here and not speak to anyone further—certainly no strangers—unless I know who they are and what they want. Do you understand, Professor?"

Satana nodded. "I understand."

"Very well. I will touch base with you later. As I said, we must push matters all the faster, now, reach full capacity by dusk."

"Full capacity?" Satana trembled. Surely, the boy was not serious. "What do you mean, full capacity?

"I mean we take matters to the ultimate level, Professor. It's what we always planned. The timeline matters little." Henry hesitated. "Are you having second thoughts?"

"No, not at all, Henry. It's just that I didn't think it would happen now—today—is all."

"Let me worry about that. You'll contact your cohorts this afternoon and explain. It's important that we stay aligned."

The boy closed the door and with his companions headed for the elevator, each feeling cruel and confident upon descent.

However, as they got off, Henry noticed the woman with the broom. As his friends gave a nod and headed outside, Henry remained rigid, studying the woman as she milled about, pretending to sweep. After a moment, her gaze fell upon him.

"Uh, hello, Mr. Hunter."

"Hello, Miss Roscoe. You look troubled."

She cracked a smile. "Troubled, Mr. Hunter? Why, I'm fine. Just thinking about what I should sweep up next."

Henry smiled. "Perhaps your thoughts."

"Excuse me?" She understood the jab, but decided it better to keep playing dumb. She tapped her ear and stretched her smile. "I didn't quite get that."

Henry looked toward the window and saw the two white-haired men and the bandana lady mumbling to one another, as if they knew something was up.

"Never mind, Miss Roscoe. I was just jesting. Do me a favor, I'd like you to visit Hawthorne Hall, let's say around one." He pointed to the window. "Please request your amiable coworkers to attend."

"But, but why, Mr. Hunter?"

She felt the intense glow of his eyes, followed by a forceful pressing upon her brow. She wobbled backward, using the broom to maintain her balance.

"Just be there, Miss Roscoe—and with your companions, as I said. I'll be none too pleased if the four of you don't show." He started to skip away, but then paused. "Oh, is the print shop open? I need to replenish my book supply."

"Yes, Mr. Hunter, it is."

"Thank you, Miss Roscoe." He gave a little wave and hopped onward. "See you soon."

She felt as though the weight of the world had been placed upon her shoulders.

"Oh, dear Lord," she muttered and stepped toward the window. Her friends sensed her gaze and upon seeing her flushed expression, trembled.

"He knows," she mouthed, as tears flowed. "He knows."

• • •

Van was still wearing his Doc Bendix disguise when he entered the Brooklyn Public Library. There was no sense in drawing attention to the famous Richard Curtis Van Loan and get folks to wondering what he was up to.

As such, he resumed the amicable, old-guy routine and culled the information he needed from various reference books and periodicals:

He learned that Satana was a renowned globetrotter of Spanish descent, though born and raised in Mexico to an affluent family with a tenuous link to rising dictator, Francisco Franco. After receiving his doctorate at Oxford, Satana made the rounds in the Soviet Union, Germany and China before landing in the Chambersburg borough of Trenton, New Jersey to stake a tutorial jaunt, only then to be run out by parents when they discovered their children's remediation had been eclipsed by dubious, ideological direction.

On the more intrinsic range, Satana was known to favor anomalous, cultural lore and endorsed both a commoner and dictatorial vantage, believing that only an urbane group could lead the lower ranks to prosperity, which otherwise meant he believed certain individuals should be curbed and contained by bureaucratic restrictions: a two-face advocacy that Van found despicable.

As for the *Master Youths of Janus*, the lofty label was absent from all reachable sources. There was, however, minor reference to a youth organization that was to be funded by an array of academic institutions, with impoverished and wayward students to be recruited through orphanages, runaway hubs and reform schools if the students passed grueling, aptitude tests. As long as the youths were bright and angst-ridden, the door would open to them. Alas, the funds to sustain such a vast network fell short, leaving only a few of Raybel's avid staff to express interest in fulfilling the deed, with "anthropological humanitarian" Ruben Satana chosen to helm it.

As to what led the selected children to adapt their militant mode was hard to say. However, a tongue-in-cheek reference in the two-year-old *Raybel Humor Magazine* did jest about Satana's discovery of strange, Mayan minerals east of the pyramids and that these disinterred samples were being delivered to Raybel for "an analysis of their mind-expanding properties." That alone spoke volumes, even if the situation's core was still bracketed in ambiguity.

After a few hours of research, Van returned to his Dusenberg to remove his makeup and though despite its roomy confines, the rearview mirror proved awkward. He cursed as he pulled off the rubber strips and removed his wig and beard, folding them like handkerchiefs (never an easy task), ruminating on what might be transpiring in the grand scheme of things. He then decided to clear his head by trekking to Lannigan's to fill his tank.

As he pulled in, his buddy popped from the garage, his smiling face full of smudges. "So how's that investigation going?"

Van rolled down his window. "Okay, I suppose. Say, would you fill 'er up, Jer?"

"Be happy to," Lannigan skipped toward the pump. "Those crazy kids have sure tapered off, but I got something you'll find of interest, something they're connected to."

"You don't say."

"Yeah, went to the newsstand to grab the afternoon *Clarion* when I spotted another book. The vendor actually had a bunch of them on display—two volumes with a possible third on the way, the guy said. He charged me a buck for it—the shyster. He was pretty enthused about an ongoing series. A genuine jerk, if ever there was one."

"I'll compensate you," Van promised. "When you're done filling, I'll park on the side. You can show me the book."

The two entered the garage. The book was on Lannigan's workbench, atop some wrenches. Van picked it up and studied the baby-blue cover. Its inked image featured the hovering Henry facing a brawny, fist-poised fellow in a skull cap marked by a large star and Old Glory emblazoned on his chest. The script read: SECOND EXCITING ISSUE! THE MASTER YOUTHS VS THE CONNIVING CAPTAIN GLORY!

"This ought to be good," Van quipped and began to flip.

"More bull, eh?"

"Why would it be otherwise?" Van absorbed a portion and then read with heightened expression, "Henry Hunter descended, his faithful companions, Jimmy Johnson and Janie Sweet gliding downward with him. They were not afraid of the self-proclaimed icon, even though he threatened to thrash them. 'You will come clean, Captain Glory, for the American people deserve to know how you've beguiled them by inciting animosity overseas. Show the face beneath your zealous patriotism—the face of instigation and betrayal. War is inevitable because of you, and America will not take the blame."

Lannigan shook his head. "That for real?"

Van scanned several more pages. "Afraid so." He flipped to the final page. "Hmmm, it appears the little bastards win the day. Captain Glory is imprisoned for war crimes, and President Roosevelt apologizes to the world for our nation being too aggressive. Hitler and Mussolini express their gratitude and harmony ensues. Quite idealistic, to say the least. Too bad these kids weren't around to nip that exasperating World War in the bud. Would have saved us all a lot of grief, even if the circumvention would have squashed our friendship."

"Gotcha on that."

Van pulled out his wallet and placed his payment on Lannigan's workbench. "I appreciate the effort. I'll study this more at length when I get back to the penthouse." He glanced at his watch. "I really should get going. If all goes according to plan, I hope to have a nice, romantic evening with Muriel."

Lannigan gave him a playful nudge. "Now, that's the Dick Van Loan I know. You enjoy yourself, tiger."

"I do intend to." Van headed off with fingers crossed.

• • •

"Just getting ready," Van explained, the receiver poised at his ear. "Oh, I would say an hour or so." He glanced at the clock. "Yes, I know I abide by a strenuous schedule, dear. Old habits die hard."

A flash of red then drew him in.

"Oh Lord, here we go." He dropped the receiver, cursed and returned it to his ear. "Sorry, there, dear." He groaned. "Oh, it's nothing, except that, well, something has come up again. Perhaps it's nothing too paramount, but all the same, I do fear I'm obligated."

He let her drone on and could not blame her for being upset. He could only hope she would understand, and if push came to shove, he could always blame her father—ha, ha.

• • •

The Phantom paced about the somber, dimly lit suite. Havens' expression fit the dolefulness.

"There are four in all—Raybel employees, custodial status—all hospitalized. One had the gumption to contact the hospital after she managed to stumble to a campus pay phone. The four were evidently left to dissipate, or worse, in an alcove at Hawthorne Hall. A chemistry chairman named Fealtor says the mishap was due to a combination of old cleaning fluids, which weakens those of mature age. The individual who called fell unconscious soon thereafter, with all four being blanketed for pickup in the courtyard. Fealtor also said the matter was rectified—swept right under the proverbial rug. Sounds real peculiar."

"Aneurysms and poisoning—those are the doctors' conjectures?"

"That's the buzz, but my sources say the docs are all over the place trying to decipher this thing. Even so, these patients are said to know something, have for a spell. In fact, they each filed complaints about activities occurring on campus, in particular at Hawthorne Hall. That's the student center. And get this. It's been since retooled for specialized, scholarly grooming for certain children. It all comes together, doesn't it? Anyway, these patients aren't in the best shape, though one—the one who called—is doing somewhat okay, coherent on occasion. It's not a coincidence that they all got struck at once and come on, by cleaning fluids?"

"Sounds like a purposeful purge."

"Like feathers have been ruffled. Well, you did say you visited the campus today. Could be the trigger."

"Yeah, that Hunter kid was wise to me. Rather telling." Van considered the matter. "Know the name of that somewhat-okay patient?"

"Sure." He picked up a sheaf of paper. "It's Miss Bridgette Roscoe. She's the one who phoned for help. She's also the one who'd know all the buildings, all the halls and any peculiar activity coming from any of them. Too bad her condition isn't conducive to questioning."

"It's Miss Bridgette Roscoe. She's the one who phoned for help."

The Phantom turned. "Let me decide that, Frank." Then in a shadowy streak, he was gone.

• • •

The old man approached the front desk and queried, "I'm here to see Miss Roscoe. I was told she's occupying one of your rooms. I'm a friend, you see, and most concerned."

"I'm sorry, sir," the pretty nurse explained, "but from what I've been instructed, she's not to be disturbed, and I'm doubtful any exceptions are to be made."

"Are you certain? I was told I could visit, that my name would be listed. I'm quite upset regarding her condition and that goes for the other staff, as well. Miss Roscoe and I are rather close, you know, and I'm a tad tense by what happened, as I'm sure you can appreciate."

The nurse smiled. "I understand, sir. Your name?"

"Paul Bendix, Dr. Paul Bendix. I'm a professor."

"Of course, at the university," the nurse continued, scanning her ledger. "My, I don't seem to see your name. I'm sorry, Dr. Bendix, but it might be better if you'd return during regular visiting hours, and perhaps by such time your name will be added to a list or you can be granted entrance by a supervisor."

"I do see, and when are your visiting hours?"

"Ten to seven daily."

"Very well. Oh, just one more thing. Might you know Miss Roscoe's room number, for when I do return, or in the very least for the sake of sending flowers?"

The nurse checked. "Room 4E. That's on the fourth floor, in the north wing. I hope that helps."

The old man smiled. "Indeed, it does, young lady. I'm most appreciative."

The old man wandered off, heading down the hall from which he had come and when out of sight, dashed into the stairwell, where he ascended like lightning to the fourth floor and then crept into the north wing.

It was quiet there, no one in sight. Nevertheless, with cat-like finesse, he passed and scanned the room numbers, gazing into a chamber that bedded two, familiar looking, white haired men, both sweaty and snoring, before coming to the door marked 4E.

He deposited his old-guy gear into his makeup case and into his green frock coat, which quasi-cloaked his belted regalia. He then donned the Phantom's signature mask. He did not intend to intimidate the woman, but once in character, he realized he might better ascertain the circumstances. Besides, the Phantom was a noted do-gooder, and his renowned persona had a far better chance of obtaining what was needed.

With soft precision, he stepped into the room. One woman appeared as stiff as a board, but breathing, albeit in a labored way. The Phantom recognized her bandana-less head and then looked to the bed across from her and spotted the broom lady, her sheet pulled up to her neck, her eyes shut, her brow pebbled in perspiration. He sensed her underlying cognition, or rather slumbered agitation, as if her fervent emotions were itching to break free.

In a voice that was husky yet consoling, the Phantom purred, "Miss Roscoe, I've come to assist. Miss Roscoe, I'm aware of your circumstances and what you reported. Would you be willing to help me, so that I may help you?" He patted her warm hand. "Please, Miss Roscoe, it is of utmost importance that we halt what is transpiring."

For a moment, she remained rigid, but then her lids quivered, cracking open to draw in his masked face.

"Do not be alarmed. I am the Phantom. I serve concerns that require justice."

"Yes, yes," she whispered, "I know of you, Phantom. I always wondered if you were real." She smiled with gratitude. "Now, I know."

"Tell me," the Phantom continued, his voice growing more sympathetic and therefore hypnotic, "who did this to you—and why?"

"It was those horrid children." Her eyes widened. "They did this to me—and my friends. Maybe we shouldn't have gone to that accursed building. Maybe we should have run away, but we're scared, didn't want to take a chance. They'd only find us anyway, we figured. That's why we went to the little room, like stupid lambs to the slaughter. We knew something was wrong there, with all that hammering and banging we'd heard, and the children coming and going as they did. Anyway, those little monsters wasted no time once we got there. They knew that we knew the truth about them—that's why they did it. Figured they get us out of the way once and for all with all those foul fumes they sprayed on us. That stupid Professor Satana is even more to blame than they are. Now even he's under their control. There are other muckety-mucks under the children's control, too—Professors Tendril and Fealtor and even the head librarian. I fear we're all doomed now, Mr. Phantom. Those vile brats are only going to grow stronger from this point on. They'll gain all the leverage."

"How could that be? No matter how crafty, they're still children." He paused, reconsidering the matter. "Tell me, Miss Roscoe, what initially prompted your suspicions? Was it simply the way they behaved or something else?"

"It was something else for sure. Ernie and Joe—the grounds supervisors—they felt it, too, so did my coworker over there, Fran. It sprung straight from Hawthorne Hall, with shady-looking workers—you know, the type that only deep pockets can buy—coming and going, carting in large pieces of wood, hammering and sawing away during all odd hours. Oh, when they weren't there, the place smelled real bad, worse than the chemistry lab ever did, like death warmed over, and the children would go to the place, sometimes lining up to get in, like they were going to get some darn vaccine, but I know they were breathing into jars, topped by these rubber cups—cups that would slip right over the nose. I asked if I might go in there and clean up, hoping I could get a glimpse of whatever was going on, but they wouldn't allow it. There was always this big guard standing by to scoot me away. My friends and I informed the faculty of the situation, but what did they care? From the president right down to the chairmen, they were all so nonchalant. None cared."

"I'm sorry to hear. Sounds terrible."

"Let's put it this way, Mr. Phantom. This group—the very foundation of that wretched institute—is corrupt to the bone. One can't believe anything that comes out of it. Do you know what those little monsters promised me? They promised they'd reveal me as the author of their stories, give me all kinds of publicity and riches to push their scam. It was all a lie, of course, to try to get me on board, keep me content. I never wanted what they were selling. I knew it was wrong. All four of us knew it. Maybe we should have gone to the police, to the Clarion, but we figured what was the point? Who'd listen? Who'd believe? I saw how Henry treated Satana yesterday in the courtyard, and that was just the start. Before they poisoned us, Henry mentioned something about finalizing matters. I remember it distinctly. I dread to think what he's up to."

"I promise I'll find out, Miss Roscoe. I thank you for your time and insight. Now please close your eyes and get your rest. I'll take it from here."

She did as requested, her expression softening. He then stepped from the room and into the hall, slipping undetected through a side door and ultimately into the springtime twilight, dashing a few blocks to his Cadillac (he did like to switch up his cars) and grabbed the Captain Glory edition from the passenger seat.

He flipped to a passage and murmured, "The Master Youths inhaled the chemicals, the flagrant minerals filling their nostrils and then their lungs, allowing them to soar like doves, but the narrow-minded Captain could not withstand the scent. His legs buckled, and he wavered backward, as the youths swarmed inward, latching onto his mind, placing it as if in a vice, squeezing as he choked and weakened." Van tossed the book back onto the seat and grimaced. "This is going to be tricky one, all right, real tricky."

He reeved the engine and pulled out, determined to thwart whatever unsavory thing the clever Henry Hunter wished to finalize, but first he would return to his penthouse to grab something from his closet of wonders.

• • •

A fierce, yellowy orange light seeped through the door of the room adjacent to Hawthorne Hall's prime expanse. A stink followed, but the four seated within the tight confines tolerated it, if only in anticipation of the promised proceedings. The four were nervous and numbed, hopeful yet fearful that the process would reach unadulterated fruition.

"Of course, with the boy," remarked Professor Fealtor, the portly science chairman, "anything is possible." He fought back a yawn. "He's the standout among them, their star, if you will, considering how he's surpassed them all. It shows in his features, in his actions. The others are loyal to his commands and each as impulsive when it comes to promoting the agenda."

"And why is that a bad thing?" the prudish Miss Pullins asked with a wearisome squirm. "They have the right purpose and plan at hand, no matter how reckless their actions may appear."

"You're only saying that," Professor Tindrell, the gangling Psychology Dean interjected with a heavy sigh, "because they've chosen you as their promotional author. You'll no doubt earn a fair sum of change when the anonymous label is lifted. There you'll be, the humble, silver-haired librarian who concocted a saga of super children, though all based on actual abilities. How inspiring."

"Better me at the helm than having a colored woman gain the fame. Was that even a consideration?"

"I think the boy likes to toy," Tindrell conjectured.

"As he perhaps should," Miss Pullins countered. "It keeps us on our toes, and despite it all, these children will show us the way. They'll live long, fruitful lives, inspiring the masses for decades. Of that, there is no question." She looked to Satana, who sat slumped across from her. "Isn't that right? You should know better than anyone."

"Yes, that's right," Satana mumbled, forcing himself from his chair with the leverage of his cane. "The children are shrewd and developing fast. Too bad we can't handle the chemical saturation as well as them." With a few clips of his cane, he hobbled to the door and placed his palm upon it. "At least the juices are cooking. I can feel it. Henry will let us know when it's done." He whiffed the stench. "We might as well prepare for it, consume the air now as well as we can. It'll sting the eyes a bit, most likely cause our noses to run, but that should be the extent."

Satana's companions felt reassured, but the professor's eyes began to tear, not from the trickling fumes, but from a deep-seated fear.

• • •

The Phantom hit a side button and watched his closet slide inward, revealing another within, though this one more capacious. He rummaged through his wardrobe and among it grabbed one esoteric item after the other. "Where is it now?" He spotted an oversized, creased, shipping envelope. "Ah, yes—Eureka!"

He opened it and removed a thin, silvery, long-sleeve smock and pants (for all perceived purposes, cosmic pajamas). He had procured the set through a banished government employee with shady underground dealings. The fabric was radiation proof (as Van confirmed through testing), among other ballyhooed assertions yet to be ascertained. Whether the fabric worked (or would work in the precise situation he hoped), he could only surmise, but even with its unavoidable equivocation, he was glad to possess it.

He got undressed, put on the burnished undergarments and then redonned his trousers and belted coat over such. He then snatched a compact gas mask from a side sshelf: one that covered just the mouth and nose. From there, he dashed to his elevator, and within seconds, was back in his Cadillac and on the road.

• • •

"Increments—that's the proper progression," Fealtor told Satana. "I hope there's nothing wrong." He glanced at his watch. "How could there not be? For all of their increased intellect, you'd think they'd know the dangers of pushing the process in one session." He pointed at the door. "The seeping looks thicker and that horrid scent is stronger." He pointed then at Tendrill. "I blame you for this. All those pats on the back without any ounce of caution—a heedless move—not to mention the grave impatience you instilled in them."

"Oh, so you're going to blame me?" Tendrill countered. "Considering how your biochemical practices set them on this reckless course. Caution was never a viable component." He studied the seeping smoke. "And who knows? At this point, they might have even extinguished themselves. Our efforts will truly be all for naught."

Satana, who had remained near the door, smiled. "Yes, extinguished themselves—that is a possibility, isn't it, if only due to the length of time? No sound. No word. Just random vibrations. Maybe it's over."

"I can't believe what I'm hearing?" Pullins wailed. "They were made to lead the way and by our solemn choice. I'm certain they know what they're doing, and it will be for the absolute best. Besides, I've no objections to waiting, especially if the outcome proves as historic as young Mr. Hunter has conveyed." She grinned like a cat having swallowed a canary. "I wonder if the children would allow me to contribute some concepts to their series. I don't see why not. I am a librarian, after all. I know a great deal of material that's perfect for plagiarizing, and it can be done in such a way to avoid lawsuits. I do happen to know a few lawyers."

"Why not steal from *Mein Kampf*?" Tindrell suggested. "As I recall, you looked quite proud of yourself in that photo from last year's book fair. You know the one, right? The one where you're grinning from ear to ear and coddling the text full front and center. And if Adolf should sue, you can just contact those lawyers."

"Very funny, but your reference isn't too far off track. What do you think those precious booklets are advocating, Professor Tindrell? It might suit you to pay better attention to the power of mass mesmerism. I'd have thought more from one of your specialized caliber."

There came a shuffling from behind the door, capped by murmuring. Again, Satana placed his palm to the door. "I've a suspicion that for better or worse, it may be time." The knob turned, and he looked back at his companions, relaying an empathetic frown to Fealtor and Tindrell. "Well, so much for extinguished prospects."

With a slow, ominous creak, the door opened, giving way to a burst of garish smoke.

Satana backed up and wavered. His colleagues followed suit, teetering and tottering and then grabbing onto one another, so as not to tumble, though perhaps more by accident than plan, they all stumbled into the main chamber, the door slamming behind them.

They were so blinded by the blistering glow and choking stench that panic set in, but no sooner had the combination struck, the hall's details came to view via a vast, twinkling outline.

The quartet noticed that the chamber's center had become consumed by a swirling pool from which a soupy, yellowy orange steamed, and atop it—floating like big-eyed angels—Henry Hunter and to each side of him, a pint-size general, albeit a few notches lower than his perch.

Against the far wall other spiffy children appeared to float, as stoic and ethereal as their leaders.

"Why they're floating, aren't they?" Fealtor stammered, giving Satana a poke, as the fumes shrouded his nostrils and eyes. "Do you see it? How can it be? It's, it's in complete emulation of those damn books."

"You're the one who enhanced the chemicals," Satana reminded him. "I only ignited those Mayan minerals from the canisters for hopeful effect, but as unique as the content is or any solution might be, I don't see how it could go this far. I do believe we're witnessing a supreme case of mind over matter, perhaps a placebo effect pushed to the extreme. Most impressive. And if my guess is right, they could reach higher heights solely through focused desire."

"No, no," Fealtor whispered into Satana's ear, growing evermore manic from the fumes, "it's more than that, Ruben, far more. I put a ton of time and effort into the formula, even worked at length with the boy genius to perfect it. I only wish we had been allowed to keep coming to the hall. He must have concocted something more. It wasn't right that we be kept away. The boy—his inflating intellect—is the key here and maybe our biggest blessing or determent. Even the smartest individuals can be unheeding. The bungled outcome with that inquisitive custodial crew proves it in spades. Anyhow, our masterful youths have been adamant about achieving transcendental flight. Henry was wise to the fact that children don't weigh much. The chemical combination could lift them, give them buoyancy, and when such would be matched by the ideal, hallucinogenic conditions—"

"Hush already, you garrulous fool," Henry hollered, causing Fealtor to swallow a thicker flow of fumes. The chairman clutched his throat and gagged. "Don't you realize my hearing is exceptional? I could hear a pin drop if I should so choose."

Santana trembled and stepped away from his colleague, suspecting he might be next, but as Fealtor hit the foggy floor, Henry looked upon his benefactor and proclaimed, "Mind over matter is, without any doubt, the essential thrust, Professor Satana. It's what makes the magic happen." The ceiling rumbled. The walls shook. "It's what gives us the right to rule—gods plucked from out the guises of babes—Janus personified and glorified to the magnanimous maximum, and all thanks to you, dear sir."

"You're, you're welcome, Henry." Santana's gut tightened, as Fealtor continued to groan. "I, uh, do appreciate it. I appreciate it very much."

"Oh, and sorry for my testiness." The boy looked to Tindrell and Pullins. "It's only due to matters being forced beyond anticipation. We've been found out, as our luck would have it. The man who approached me on the corner today was the same who visited Professor Satana a few hours later: a different look, but the same man. I wonder who may have given him the incentive to probe our cause and rush us onward." He looked down at Fealtor and then back to Tindrell and Pullins. "Would it be our fallen compatriot or perhaps, just perhaps, one of you?"

"It's certainly not me," Pullins cried.

"Nor I," Tindrell protested. "I worked with you children, nurtured you to believe in yourselves, to expand your collective perception." He then hushed, fearful he had said too much.

"I am only teasing, Professor Tindrill. I realize that neither of you could be so deceitful. Perhaps it was only inevitable that we would be sought out, with us making the rounds as we did, but Professor Satana assured us that to implement our goal, we only needed to roam, share our goods, collect our donations, plant our seeds and above all, concentrate. To concentrate is most important." The boy dipped (or perhaps more so, crouched), motioning to his generals. "Concentration is what made us evolve. It came from you good people and the exotic materials you asked us to inhale. Then the results rose from within us, from out our minds, where all great things transpire. That's how the words came, how my stories were built." He gestured to the brown-haired boy. "That's how Jimmy came to illustrate." He gestured to the red-haired girl. "And how Janie found the means to design and bind." He turned to the boys and girls against the wall. "It's how we became so perfectly, idealistically aligned, with a cloaked agenda ready to spring and infiltrate, merged as one from an array of mythologies, so tight, so impenetrable, so cruel yet kind." He laughed to the point that the sinister sound echoed, seeming to cause the ceiling to crack and spread a tad further. "Behold, my poor, mature plebeians, at what you've conjured. Behold—the Master Youths of Janus!"

Pullins was tempted to make the sign of the cross, only then to remember that she was above that sort of thing. Still, the boy's boldness had unsettled her, and the same went for Tindrell, who quaked in his boots and nibbled at his nails, awaiting the next dictatorial blow. Satana, meanwhile, stood cautious, wondering which way the tide would turn.

Hawhthorne Hall rumbled again. The untamed, chemical light grew brighter, swooshing from the floor up to the ceiling.

The backdrop children hopped about the air in eerie place, clapping, giggling, as Henry, Janie and Jimmy held stoic court as the radiating fumes twirled ever faster.

Satana now sensed danger and with frantic flair beseeched, "Stop it—stop it now. It's getting out of hand," but it was too late. The chaotic process was hitting its maddening summit.

• • •

The Phantom parked his Cadillac alongside a couple of towering trees, a decent distance from the streetlights and leapt toward the campus' steel-arched gateway.

The distant view of Hawthorne Hall looked like a volcano ready to burst. Even the twilight sky looked ruddy from its violate warmth.

The big guard from earlier noticed his approach and blocked his passage. "Hey, Buster, no one gets in without a pass."

"Do tell. Since when?"

"This afternoon." The guard edged nearer to see if the man before him really wore a mask. He laughed. "Maybe you should be heading off to a masquerade instead."

"*Au contraire*," the Phantom replied with a sarcastic sneer, "I do believe the masquerade is happening right here."

The Phantom then delivered a few quick blows to the big man's abdomen and neck, reducing the goon to flaccid form. He skipped over the unconscious oaf, only to notice more guards prancing about the courtyard, but they were too preoccupied with the impetuous light that spewed from the building's spacious windows.

Students zigzagged before the phenomenon, exchanging a barrage of frantic speculations.

"Got to get inside," the Phantom whispered. "It'll be tricky, though. The phenomenon seems to be brewing on the lower level and rising from there."

He strapped on his gas mask, yanked the collar of his undergarment toward his chin. He recalled that the fabric's protective flow was supposed to extend beyond the neck. Then again, how could he be certain? Also, though the gas mask would help, it would only cover a portion of his face. Though he had his knife in his sleeve and his .45 automatic in his coat, what good would either do against this unknown glow? He might be facing full, lethal infection by plunging forth.

He decided to toss caution to the wind and with great zeal jaunted toward Hawthorne Hall, much to the shock of the wary bystanders, who questioned what sort of fool would dare approach such evident doom. Nonetheless, he reached the threshold within seconds. He tried to open the doors, but they seemed stuck by whatever weird residue spewed from within, and so with deft precision thrust his shoulder against the wood.

After a few ardent tries, the doors snapped inward, and a hot, luminous haze rolled outward. The bystanders gasped and oohed, backing farther away to huddle and point. The Phantom dashed in, expecting the worse.

At first his vision became blurred, but he forced his eyes to adjust and in glancing upward, noticed a youth stationed above.

Whether the boy actually hovered or was but a mere projected illusion was hard to say. Even so, there he was, Henry Hunter, levitating with airplaned arms, his nose pointed upward like some erudite angel, his insidious compatriots at each side, emulating his aeronautic stance. Other children, about the same age and a dozen in total, bounced behind the three as if riding the yellowy orange waves, emitting a crotchety euphoria that punctuated their censorious creed.

On the floor, a portly man rose, but at best managed only to sit up. Another man, gangling and ashen, trembled off to the side. On the other end, a woman pulled at her hair, smiling yet crying: insanity personified.

It was obvious that the whole sector had been gassed to the hilt, not unlike in those horrendous moments he had experienced during the war, and yet this was something altogether different. The surrounding substance may have been eroding the foundation, but was a chemical, no matter how strong, capable of that?

The Phantom then recalled what Miss Roscoe had said about workers coming and going at Hawthorne Hall. Perhaps their tinkering had weakened the structure, the chemicals only adding fuel to the fire.

"Who's that there?" the smug Henry Hunter inquired, scanning the Phantom's willowy shape. "Step into view. I want to see you. We all want to see you."

The other children slowed their tick-tocking sways, looking down at the churning floor.

The Phantom turned in response, only to notice Satana, whose eyes beamed with confounded dread and exhaustion. He stirred his cane about the mist, as if tunneling a path, and picked up pace.

"You heard the boy. Who are you?" Satana croaked. "Do I know you? You look rather famil—"

To intercede, Henry leapt from one smoky stretch to another, and then onto another after that, scooting forward to stretch his leg and more by accident than plan, grazed Satana's brow with a cut of his wee heel. The boy mumbled his disdain, for the Phantom was the one he had wished to strike, if only to get a better view of the man's face.

"Yes, you do look familiar," the disgruntled lad accused, then deciding to abandon his descent and pulled himself up, as if by his fingertips, and with acrobatic finesse he moved onto a higher cloud, only to repeat the gesture to reach yet another smoky stretch, until he regained his lofty position. He swiveled with pixie-like buoyancy (no doubt abetted by the lightened atmosphere) and again pointed down. "I know you from the contours of your face. You're the same man third time over, now in another disguise—a prominent disguise, even if spoiled by that obscuring gas mask." He laughed. "I've seen your face in *the Clarion*, from all those blurry shots that people captured after you allegedly saved the day. You're the one that Manhattan's citizens speak of with bated breath—the Phantom!"

"You got that right, Sonny," the Phantom confirmed. "Say, why don't you come back down and give me another try."

The boy clapped with obstinate glee. "How bold of you, but boldness will

"I know you from the contours of your face."

matter little when you succumb like these others. You'll do our bidding and give us whatever we want."

"These others, you say? You mean the adults?" He pointed to Satana, who rubbed his jaw, struggling to stay balanced. The Phantom then gestured to Fealtor, Tendrill and Pullins, who appeared even more despondent. "Do you really want to betray those who placed you upon your lofty pedestal?"

"He would do no such thing," Pullins choked. She looked up at Henry with hands pressed. "We've an agreement. It's all to be revealed. I'm Anonymous, if only for now. Mr. Hunter's to make my name known to all the world and—"

"Silence, woman!" Henry roared.

"But I'm, I'm on your side—here to help you, Mister Hunter. We're, we're all here to help. You have our complete obedience—anything you want, but we only ask for a few minor things in return, now that the next phase is complete, all based on our agreement."

"You have all you need," the boy berated. "Now it is your turn to give—and give all that you can."

The Phantom pointed at the boy and guffawed. "So that's how you treat those who made you? You clam them up and ask for more?"

Henry glowered at the Phantom. "You make a bold presumption, sir. You should know, it's all a matter of perspective of who created whom. My quest for greatness always lurked beneath my spry guise. The same goes for all the children here. Who's to say that we didn't pull these adults into our collective subconscious to do our bidding, to make us their superiors? Perhaps they even wished to make us their rulers. If so, their wish has been granted."

"Maybe you're right. Maybe that's what they wanted, but I'm of a different ilk, Henry Hunter. I've no desire to be enslaved."

"You get bolder still, Phantom," the youth assessed. "I dare say, you'll make a worthy villain for Volume Three—the *Vile Phantom vs the Master Youths of Janus*. I believe it'll be our best yet."

"Especially if readers see you for what you are. I'm certain they'll take great delight in your demise—administered by me."

The rebuttal offended Henry, whose face turned gremlin-like. "You'd be wise to watch your tone."

"And if I don't, what will you do, swoop down and graze my brow? Feel free, young man. I told you, I welcome the altercation."

"Don't provoke him," Satana warned, gurgled fumes seeping past his lips. "The boy has no mercy."

"I'll take my chances," the Phantom replied. "Come on, boy. Let's see what you've got."

The Phantom's audacity startled the boy. However, instead of descending, he stretched his arms once more in airplaned fashion and twirled them: a silly gesture at the outset, but the gaseous strands soon stirred, generating circles within circles, the effect becoming all the more celestial, as if some great sorcerer was at task. Then with an energetic thrust, the boy snapped his arms forward, and with this, chemical streams smacked upon the Phantom's chest.

The vibrating impact made the Phantom reel and Satana tumble. However, the Phantom managed to dig in his heels, the creamy residue skidding off his coat like a sideway spray of rain.

Santana stayed floored within the unstable glow, as broken as his colleagues, who coughed and slid farther back, even more distressed than before, their faces drained of what little vim they had yet held.

The Phantom laughed harder. "Is that all you got, boy?" He pounded his chest. "Go on. Try again."

Jimmy and Janie looked upon their leader. The children behind them murmured in confusion and doubt. Henry was at a loss for words, and because of it, his angst mounted.

Again he twirled his arms, looking to his generals to simulate the gesture, and as they complied, those behind them did the same. The collective filled the atmosphere with spirals of rich, autumnal hues, the fumes' impact flattening Fealtor, Tendrill and Pullins, their backs flat to the floor, gasping in vain for clear air.

All the while the Phantom stood impervious despite the steady discharge, and the panic-stricken Henry could not figure how or why.

"It isn't working," Janie wailed.

"He's not even flinching," Jimmy screeched.

"Press on," Henry insisted. "I insist—press on."

Try as they may, the duo fell short, their arms falling to their sides: an act that proved contagious enough to leave the other children rigid and blank. The circles ebbed and soon swung without purpose.

Henry looked upon his compatriots' abandonment in horror, his lips quivering, his cheeks reddening in shame.

"No, no, no—you can't give up. It goes against the grain. It goes against all that we're meant to be and do."

The Phantom laughed harder, louder. "It appears a new face emerges," he chided, "a face of a little boy with illusions of grandeur, but in the end, he turned out to be a fake. In fact, this whole, elaborate scenario is fake."

The children in the backdrop began to flop and skid upon their makeshift clouds, but the truth behind the illusion became succinct when Janie and Jimmy sat in defeat, letting their legs dangle from their extended planks, which grew more apparent within the thinning fumes.

"No, no, no—you're wrong, wrong, wrong," Henry stammered, stomping upon the centered tongue of wood that stretched from out the rear wall. "I'm not a fake. I'm real, real, real."

Santana hoisted his cane from the pool in which he wallowed and declared, "You have failed, Henry Hunter—failed yourself—failed us all, as we have failed you." He pushed himself up, his legs bending and wobbling in the process. "This whole, egomaniacal experiment, it was a major mistake, rushed to the point of becoming this catastrophic blunder. Intellect alone does not make one a god. You were smart enough to know that, but that, in itself, is no cause to rejoice." He glanced at the Phantom. "Be glad this farce has been exposed. Be glad this phase is over."

"No, no, no," the boy persisted, teetering at the plank's edge. "We achieved what we needed. We reached the highest level we could—that anyone could. You know it, too. You're a liar to say otherwise. A liar, you hear?" He shook his fists and flailed. "A stupid liar—"

Henry then lost his footing. The children gasped and screamed as he fell, expecting the worst, but the agile Phantom leapt with astounding grace, catching the boy in his arms.

Henry groaned and looked into the masked man's penetrating eyes and fainted.

With the boy cradled, the Phantom bolted to the door. He had to leak the fumes, but Satana interceded by swinging his cane before them.

"Allow me. You check my colleagues—see that they're conscious and if not, so be it."

Satana's cold tone unnerved the Phantom, but he quickly made the rounds, bending with the boy to inspect the professor's peers: each at this point unconscious yet breathing, but for how much longer?

He then re-stationed himself before the children, taking in their frigid faces.

"So, what do you say for yourselves?" the Phantom asked. "Come now—speak up."

Jimmy shrugged. "What's there to say?" He looked about. "It's over. That's all."

Janie shrugged, too. "That's right—all over. There's nothing more to do."

The youngsters behind them remained unflinching, though a few found the gumption to slide down the adjoining shoots or reach nearby ladders, swooshing away yellow streaks and orange plumes, clumsy and hard in their descending gaits, now purged of their minor, gaseous buoyancy.

They also appeared at enormous ease with their surreal habitat: a convex contortion that may have passed for a reassembled squid, as slithers of moonlight bled through the ceiling cracks, pouring upon sideline canisters, some of which still seeped the colorful gas with hints of inner flames. Near them were several trash cans, brimming of those rubber-capped jars that Miss Roscoe had referenced.

The scene's sardonic serenity infuriated the Phantom, but it enraged him more that the children were so lackadaisical about it. Did they truly think it normal?

"So, that's all you have to say? It's over? There's nothing more to it?" He lifted the limp boy. "Don't you care about your leader? For all you know, the poor boy might be dead."

"His chest is heaving," Jimmy stated. "That means he's breathing."

"And there's still color in his cheeks," Janie added. "I can see from here. He's alright. Why fret?" She waved her finger at the three, despondent scholars. "He's definitely in better shape than they are. They're a step away from being dead."

The Phantom quaked with rage, thus rattling the boy, who moaned, his eyelids twitching. The Phantom pressed him close to his chest and tapped his cheek. "That's it. Snap out of it, son. Wake up."

Henry writhed, insinuating a need to break free, but as much as he appeared perturbed, a repentant expression rose.

"I didn't mean it," he whispered. "I promise I won't steal any more bicycles. I promise. Just put me back in the reform school. Please, mister, please." His eyes teared, and then he paused and squinted drowsily. "Say, why you wearing that mask, the one over your eyes?" He looked frightened. "You a burglar, a robber?"

"No, not in the least," the Phantom explained. He pulled off his gas mask, so that the gamut of his alter ego could been seen. "In fact, I help people, and the mask I'm wearing symbolizes that fact."

Janie and Jimmy absorbed the exchange with keen interest. The others also pricked up their ears.

"Help people?" Henry's voice grew louder. "People like me?"

"Yes, like you." The Phantom smiled. "I help people who've been hurt, abused, led astray." His smile widened. "I set wrongs right. My name is the Phantom. Maybe you've heard of me."

The children caught on and chanted his name, for it rang with truth and hope: "Phantom, Phantom, Phantom."

Fealtor flopped about like a fish out of water, made cognitive by the chorus. "We helped them—the selfish, little fools. We helped each and every one of them." He sprung up, shaking all the while. "We made them better than they could ever hope to be. They know it, too."

Upon hearing Fealtor's voice, Tendrill stirred, sitting upward and declaring, "He's right. We expanded their minds, gave them the focus and confidence they needed."

Pullins sat up as well, pointing at the Phantom. "Your sort would only keep them shackled, without any chance to rise, to lead. They'll come to understand that. They must."

Satana then clicked back into view, prompting the chants to fade. He paused a few feet from the Phantom and Henry and then turned to each of his cohorts.

"I see you've each survived, but that doesn't mean you've pulled through with any sense. We did not help these children, not in the least. We did not help ourselves or any great cause. Our experiment was an abject failure." His eyes moved to Henry. "They only learned to fabricate their greatness. The chemical inhalations prove nothing. These children were only tricked into thinking they were gods. They emerged as little charlatans who wished to frighten us into harnessing more funds to produce more propaganda. That crazed wall of preposterous planks says it all." His eyes rolled back to the Phantom. "That's not the shared countenance we wished them to bear. We truly wanted these children be more than they are. We wanted them to be immortal, or at least something akin to it." He turned to his aborted, gawking creations. "We will try again. We will learn from our mistakes and grow—grow until we gain the success, the veritable power—they were meant to attain."

"If that's what you believe," the Phantom retorted, his voice thick and ominous, "then you've learned nothing."

Satana shot him a vile look. "What do you know of learning? Look at you. You're no different than them, than any of us here. You're nothing but an impulsive masquerader. But we have the backbone to open the gateway. Whether child or adult, we will pull from our psyches the strength to fix this world for the better." He notched his arm upward. "Whether you wish to accept it or not, a new world order is upon us." His arm stiffened into a sinister salute. "Hail—the Master Youths of Janus. The children shall lead us into a new, golden age."

An eerie silence fell upon the chamber and then from the Phantom's arms, the boy sprung onto Satana. The two fell to the floor, the boy kicking, punching and yelling, "I hate you—hate you. You're nothin' but a dirty, rotten, two-faced fink, and the Master Youths are all fakes. You hear me? Fake, fake, fake. You hear?"

The Phantom pulled the boy off Satana, though his spindly limbs yet flailed with an avidity to reattack.

"Fake, fake, fake," Henry continued, and in little time, the others joined in with great vigor, "Fake, fake, fake."

Satana remained on the floor, nurturing a broken smile, while Fealtor, Tendrill and Pullins shook their fists and clucked their tongues with as much incentive as their frail frames would permit. Nothing they could say or do mattered now, especially when the whirling sound of sirens hailed from outside, drowning the chant to a restive hush.

A bleary-eyed, young policeman appeared, hand over his mouth, mumbling, "Just got here. Sorry for the delay. The courtyard's filled with officers and firemen, all set to help. We got ambulances, too." The officer looked at the children, watching as more descended their crescent platforms, Janie and Jimmy leading the way. "I guess whatever happened in here is pretty much over, right?"

"Yeah, in a sense," the Phantom answered. He pointed to the flaccid Satana and his trio. "But it truly isn't over until justice is served."

More police, accompanied by firefighters, swept in, gathering the children and ushering them outside. A couple policemen lifted Satana, and a few others took hold of his colleagues.

"You might want to keep an eye on that group," the Phantom recommended. "They have a lot of explaining to do."

The officers nodded and escorted the weary masterminds from Hawthorne Hall, with Pullins mustering before exiting, "They promised me I would get credit. I am Anonymous, you know. I am Anonymous."

Havers gave the woman a perplexed glance as he made his way in, looking spiffy and content despite the handkerchief balled at his nose. He gazed up at the crumbling ceiling and the canisters, then the boy and last but not least, the Phantom.

"I knew you'd be here." He lowered his handkerchief, his nostrils shifting fast to accommodate the residual scent. "I caught word of how bad things had gotten from my sources. Quite a catastrophe we have here." He pulled out a pen and pad from his inner, jacket pocket. "Why don't you give me the scoop? I've no doubt it's a ripe one."

The Phantom tucked his protruding, silver collar downward, wiped his neck and grinned. "Ready if you are, friend."

• • •

The Phantom shared all the details, even though there was still much to theorize upon, in particular why the institute's staff would embark on such a dangerous and unethical endeavor. After all, children were involved. Henry remained at the Phantom's side throughout, weakened and teary, until it was decided he would be better off going to the hospital with the other children for observation. There was no telling how deep the gaseous effects had extended.

"We need buses," the Phantom stated. "There are too many kids—too many people here in general—to be checked. No matter how many ambulances and vehicles you've got, they can't handle them all."

Havens darted over to a group of officers and explained the situation, who then headed off, obviously following through. When he returned to the Phantom, he asked, "So that spaceman suit—it really helped?"

"Seems so, along with my trusty gas mask. I donned the gear based on information Miss Roscoe gave me. The fabric is supposed to be repellent to a number of substances. I figured it couldn't hurt to sport it. I only hope the residue doesn't do any long-term damage to you or the others here, though I'm confident it's thinned out pretty well by now."

"It is what it is," Havens remarked, looking about. "Amazing construction and awfully weird." He studied the gamut of the curled ramps and perches. "But to take pride in pulling the wool over people's eyes—what kind of genius is that?"

"I suppose even little geniuses tend to look at things from a playful view," the Phantom postulated. "Poor kids. Despite it all, they're a sad, impoverished lot. The fault lies in those who pulled their strings. Funny that their manipulators had their strings pulled in turn. What strange irony, not to mention quite a disparaging outcome for all involved. Arrests will be made, no doubt."

"No doubt." Havens scribbled further. "I'll take great pleasure in headlining this to the hilt and of course, based solely on the facts."

"I wonder if the readership will believe those facts. This will be one wild account."

"I'll let it fall where it will. The same goes for Raybel's reputation. There won't be a need to editorialize much, either. If *the Clarion* should tarnish the institution's luster for the long haul, then I've done my job. It's the faculty's fault this happened. Radicalism never works, no matter how the propaganda is gift-wrapped."

• • •

Muriel looked quite fetching in her snug, red dress as she spread the typed pages across the coffee table.

"Got two stories done. Cleaned up the syntax. Hope you don't mind. Also, your handwriting is quite atrocious. Even so, I wanted to show you what I've done so far, at least on those particular evenings when you've been too busy."

Van flopped on the sofa and edged toward her. "I told you there was no rush. It's all frivolous, my dear, pure self-indulgence."

"Like those *Master Youths of Janus* books?"

He frowned. "Yeah, sort of." He contemplated the matter. "You know, now that you mention it, maybe it's better to put all that fictional memoir mish-mash on the backburner."

"I won't argue the point. Some of that stuff is pretty far-fetched. At the rate it was going, I'd expect you—or whoever this sleuth alter ego is—to team up with Captain Glory somewhere down the line."

Van raised a finger. "Ah, Glory is supposed to be a bad guy, remember?"

"I doubt that very much. Anyone who'd oppose those obnoxious children—well, let's just say I got the gist of their double-dealing."

"I'm just glad they're doing okay now, Henry in particular. His features are softening, and he's already back to studying, engaging in creative writing and the like, though nowhere as advanced as he was. He'll progress over time, in a natural way, especially if his guilt-ridden parents have any say in the matter. It appears that social workers are also getting the others back in order at their various bases. A most promising sign, despite the pain and confusion that comes with intense withdraw."

"And what of their victims, those poor people from the maintenance crew?"

"Yes, the crew." Van folded his hands. "I hear Bridgette Roscoe is set to return to work soon. Her coworkers are bouncing back, as well. The gaseous influence and the traces of hypnotic control have fled, all gone like a bad dream. Oh, and a class-action lawsuit against Raybel is pending, but I bet our friends will do just dandy after the dust clears. I've no doubt your father will love covering that. Anyhow, they can presently take delight in knowing that the pompous Professor Satana and his crackpot cohorts are behind bars, precisely where they belong, though a shift to an institute of the criminally insane seems better suited. It'll also be interesting to decipher the exact composition of that mind-altering substance they used, especially taking into account the professed, Mayan extracts."

"I see. Indeed, so much to learn, but where does that leave you? I mean you were there when it all came to fruition, doing your playboy investigative thing, at least according to what my father informed me and of course, what hit print. I would say, no matter your carefree intent, it must have been quite a shock to the system."

"Ah, don't forget I'm a war vet. If my flights of hazardous fancy didn't toughen me up, nothing will." He loosened his smoking jacket in a subtle but suggestive way. "Besides, the situation wasn't so shocking that a little, basic comforting couldn't appease it, if you get my meaning."

Muriel paused, and her eyes grew misty. "That evening when you gave me your material—it was a ruse, wasn't it? I mean, you clearly don't care about those stories."

Without warning, he planted a kiss on her the lips that may have lasted far longer if not for that piercing, red light.

He pulled away, his lips yet puckered, but his steely gaze set beyond.

"What's wrong?" She sighed. "Oh, don't tell me. You've suddenly remembered you have something to do."

He grimaced. "Uh, how did you know?"

"It's a little more than obvious."

"Yeah, well, it may seem more than coincidental, but um, it is the truth." He tapped his temple. "Heck, the ol' memory isn't what it used to be, my dear, and uh, I do apologize—apologize from the bottom of my heart."

She gave him a sly look, not accepting the explanation, but seeing no need to overanalyze it. It was just the lay of the land with Richard Curtis Van Loan. Why fight it? She knew in her heart he was loyal to her. That more than sufficed.

"Tell you what." She stood and smoothed her dress. "At this stage of the game, why don't we compromise?" She pointed to the pages. "I quit this foolish typing gig, and maybe, just maybe, on some fleeting night, we can actually spend some decent time together—and preferably not here. For whatever odd reason, your penthouse seems to trigger these peculiar interruptions." She held out her hand. "Deal?"

He sprung up and gave her hand a dainty shake. "Deal."

They headed to the door, where he kissed her brow and apologized again for cutting the evening short.

"I'll walk you to the elevator."

"I know the way, Mr. Van Loan. I always know the way."

Then no sooner had she departed, he jaunted to his closet and grabbed his coat, fedora and from his waistband, his mask.

He strapped it on nice and tight, and then with great pride and stealth embarked on what would no doubt be another thrilling chapter.

THE END

My Phantom Challenge

It is daunting for me to write for a character I haven't tackled before, and when Ron Fortier enlisted me to compose a *Phantom Detective* yarn, based on the famous, Thrilling Publications subtitle, I got edgy. On the other hand, I got edgy when he asked me to tackle Ravenwood and the Dead Sheriff. With this in mind, I decided to do for the Phantom, aka Richard Curtis Van Loan, what I did for those other tried-and-true legends: Plunge in and not look back.

The real crust of the challenge, however, was creating the ideal exploit for our protagonist, and from there (fingers crossed) all would flow. Before long, concepts manifested.

I have always found dictators most infuriating, in particular the way they try to mold others to think as they do, based on the outlandish justification that it's all for the populace's greater good.

I also hate skewed propaganda and how it can impact the young: the Hitler Jugend being a blistering example.

In a related strand, bad-seed children (those who seem destined to worsen over time) also unsettle me. Such related stories as John Wyndham's *The Midwich Cuckoos/Village of the Damned*, Jerome Bixby's "It's a Good Life" (adapted by Rod Serling for *the Twilight Zone*) and *Brightburn* (little Kal-El in philosophical reverse) became blueprints for what I was to compose, brushed with a thick coating of Ellis St. Joseph's evolutionary *Outer Limits* episode, "The Sixth Finger."

With these influences at play, I came to shape my story and decided to implant an idea of duality (a concept I do rather fancy) for the sake of sprinkling some Jekyll/Hyde substance abuse into the plot, but also made it a point to place the circumstances' blame on its "erudite" adults. These super-pumped Fagins are responsible for pushing the children to a monstrous, backfiring fault. (In this respect, I guess there's also a dose of Mary Shelley's *Frankenstein* in the story, wherein the creations come to despise and reject their creators.)

When all was said and done, it was fun sticking Van (and for a brief stint, his WWI buddy, Jerry Lannigan) into the mad-youth predicament, where surface-value innocence is unmasked as crafty malignance. However, despite the psychedelic bracketing that infiltrates the story's later part (a huge, L. Frank Baum ruse for those in the know), I believe that "the Master Youths of Janus" surfaces as a standard, good-vs-evil parable and therefore meets the Phantom's moral mode (and code).

Hope I handled the challenge well enough to have kept readers engaged.

MICHAEL F. HOUSEL has written the following Airship 27 novels: *MARK JUSTICE'S THE DEAD SHERIFF*, VOL 4; *THE PERSONA—ENTER THE PERSONA!*; *THE PERSONA: GREEN-FLESHED FIENDS*; and *THE HYDE SEED*. He has also contributed to *RAVENWOOD, STEPSON OF MYSTERY*, VOL 4 and the upcoming VOL 5.

In addition, his work can be found in the Eighth Tower Publishing release, *THE BLACK STONE: STORIES FOR LOVECRAFTIAN SUMMONINGS* and Main Enterprises' *WHAT EVER!* magazine. One can visit his literary, film and collectible reviews at http://bizarrechats.blogspot.com/.

NINE OF YOUR BEST FRIENDS

by Fred Adams, Jr.

Soft music played on the radio as Aaron Lindsey slumped in his armchair. He was so tired that he didn't even bother to loosen his necktie. It didn't matter. He'd lost so much weight the past year working sixteen hours a day to keep his insurance business afloat that last year's suit hung on him as if it were on a wire coat hanger. His was just another struggle in the Great Depression. He'd heard FDR say on that same radio the week before that things were turning around, but that train hadn't arrived for him.

Katy, his pretty dark haired wife came in with a highball in one hand and her purse in the other. He smiled sadly. She hadn't had a new dress for almost two years, and all of her clothes were looking shabby. But she never complained. She handed him the drink. "I won't be late." She was going to play cards with some of her friends, the one entertainment that they could all afford. Lindsey was almost relieved that she was going out for the evening. He loved her company, but tonight he was just too tired to even talk.

"Enjoy yourself, honey," he said. "I'll be waiting for you when you come home."

The doorbell rang. "There's Geraldine." She pecked Lindsey on the cheek then rubbed off a dab of lipstick with her thumb. "Bye-bye."

"Bye-," Lindsey said as the front door closed behind her. He was asleep before he could finish his farewell. His head sunk on his chest and the glass tipped in his hand, pouring his drink on the carpet.

He woke with a start to stare into the eyes of a man whose coat was pulled up around his face and hat down over his brow. Lindsey couldn't breathe. The intruder had one hand on the short end of his necktie and the other on the knot, pulling it taut. He yanked the gasping Lindsey out of his chair and dragged him bodily through the doorway into the hall.

"Wha— wha—" Lindsey choked as his assailant dragged him through the kitchen and out the back door into the darkness. He flailed at his attacker, but his blows were ineffectual. He would have cried out for help but couldn't get the words out.

The man kicked the garage door open, and in the dim light from the street, Lindsey saw his shopworn Pontiac, the driver's door hanging open. "Behind the wheel," the assailant whispered in his ear. Lindsey grabbed at the steering wheel, using it to try to pull free of his attacker, but it was no use. He was just

123

too tired…too tired.

The knot tightened and Lindsey felt consciousness slipping away from him. The last thing he heard was a voice whispering, "Goodbye, Aaron."

• • •

Life really isn't so bad, Lloyd Montrose thought, jingling his keys as he climbed the steps to his front door. Plenty of people had been wiped out by the crash and the resulting Depression but he'd managed to weather it far better than most. A little luck and a little talent and a lot of fight had carried him through. It might have been different if he'd married and had children and mouths to feed, but living the solitary life allowed him to devote his life to ruthless survival.

Every day he'd walk to his office and see the poor souls in the bread lines. He patted his paunch with satisfaction. No soup kitchens for Lloyd Montrose, he thought. Like the song says, "I got my own."

He put his key in the lock and before he could turn it, the door creaked slowly inward. Across the darkened foyer Montrose saw a thin line of light under his study door. He reached down to the umbrella stand and took out a nine iron he kept by the door to discourage peddlers and beggars and crept quietly to the study. He reached a hand for the knob, the nine iron raised to club whoever was hiding on the other side. His hand touched the cold brass of the knob at the same instant he felt the cold steel of a gun barrel below his ear.

"Not a sound," a voice whispered. "Into the room."

"Look, friend," Montrose said, in a voice calmer than it should have been. "Take whatever you want. My wallet's in my hip pocket and my watch is in my vest. I have some cash in my desk drawer. I haven't seen your face. I can't identify you. Take it and go."

The hammer of the revolver clicked. "Into the room."

Montrose still held the golf club and weighed his options. If he could get a step away and the gun wasn't pressed against him, he could swing the club and maybe knock it away. He didn't survive the trenches of No Man's Land to lose it all to some punk with a two dollar pistol. He stepped through the doorway and gasped in spite of himself.

The study was ransacked; drawers spilled onto the floor, carpet pulled up, furniture overturned and paintings pulled from the walls. The intruder shoved him between his shoulders and sent him stumbling toward the desk.

He spun and swung the nine iron one handed, catching the intruder on the left temple with a glancing blow and knocking off his hat. Montrose looked to the gun and his eyes widened. The pistol was no cheap pop gun. He recognized the distinctive reptilian lines of a Luger. He'd seen enough of them in the War. His eyes drifted up to the attacker's face and gasped again. "You!"

"Surprise!"

The Luger roared and the bullet ripped through Montrose's chest. As he lay on the floor, life oozing from him, his assassin bent close to him and whispered, "Goodbye, Lloyd."

• • •

"Lovely evening, isn't it?" The sultry blonde in an off-the-shoulder gown said as she sidled up to Richard Curtis Van Loan.

"Yes," he said. "It is." He recognized her as Evelyn McBride, daughter of the steel magnate. She put a cigarette to her lips and Van reflexively reached for his lighter. Through the French doors of the penthouse balcony, a pianist deftly flirted with "I'm Confessin'" and the cocktail party guests stood or sat in small groups sipping martinis and making the Cole Porter kind of party talk that irritated Van. He'd come to the balcony overlooking Central Park for two reasons, one of them to escape the mundane banter.

He flicked his thumb and saw the lighter's flame mirrored in Evelyn's seductive hazel eyes. She breathed in and the tip of her cigarette glowed a bright orange. She breathed out and let twin streams of smoke drift from her straight, delicate nose.

Evelyn's intentions were obvious. She'd been eyeing Van from a distance all evening, watching for a chance to get him alone. The wealthy playboy was a catch coveted by many of New York's loveliest ladies, but it was to no avail. Richard Curtis Van Loan's heart belonged to another, although she'd never know it. Van was hopelessly devoted to Muriel Havens, the ember-haired daughter of his friend and confidante Frank Havens, publisher of the *Clarion*, a city daily.

Truth be told, Van could have his choice of New York's most beautiful women, but romance was not for him. Under the façade of a wealthy carefree playboy lay his secret identity, the masked crime fighter known as the Phantom Detective. He realized that anyone to whom he became close would be placed in immediate jeopardy, should his identity be discovered. So far, it remained a secret between Van and Frank, and he intended to keep it so.

"I was wondering what a girl has to do to catch your attention, Van."

He smiled and didn't answer. The last of summer twilight was fading from rose to indigo.

Evelyn took her cigarette from her mouth and closed her eyes, tipping her head and leaning in for a kiss. "I hope you aren't one of those boys who like boys."

Over her shoulder, Van saw across town, a red light at the top of a skyscraper. This was the second reason he'd come outside. The beacon was a signal that he was needed. He took a step backward, and Evelyn stumbled off balance. Her eyes popped open, this time angry.

"Sorry, Evelyn; I must excuse myself."

"You— you— "

Van stepped through the French doors and was almost to the penthouse elevator when his host, George Luyden and his wife Maude caught him by the arm.

"Not leaving so soon, are you Van?" George said. "Why, nobody's even drunk yet!" He laughed at his own joke.

"And once the first guest departs, the rest follow soon after," Maude said. "Won't you please stay a while longer?"

Van gave a rueful smile. "I wish I could, Maude, but tonight just isn't my night." He cast a look over his shoulder. George and Maude followed his gaze across the room where Evelyn stood glaring at him. The couple shared a knowing look. "Of course," Maude said. "You run along."

"Thank you for a wonderful dinner. I'll see you both soon."

At the curb, Rodney, Van's chauffeur stood talking to a knot of liveried drivers a half block away where their cars were parked. Seeing his boss exit the lobby, he climbed into the dark blue Dusenberg touring car and pulled up to the building's entrance. Van opened his own door and climbed in the front seat beside Rodney.

"You're out early," the black man said. "Boring party?"

Van shook his head. "Take me to the Clarion building, Rod." No elaboration given, none required. Van regarded Rodney as more a trusted friend than an employee, but if Rodney suspected his boss to be the Phantom Detective, he never let on.

"You got it."

Rodney swung the big Dusenberg into the street and glided away past the Park and across Manhattan. Evening traffic was light and in a few minutes Van stepped out of the car at the revolving doors of the Clarion Building. The sidewalks were empty except for a few men and women coming to or going from work. Inside the building he would have never known that it was night.

A daily newspaper never sleeps. People bustled around as if it were noon, preparing the next day's edition. At the reception desk, a uniformed guard stood as Van approached. "Good evening, Mister Van Loan."

"Good evening, Albert."

"Mister Havens is expecting you." He rang upstairs to announce Van's arrival and picked up a ring of keys then led Van across the lobby to Frank Havens' private elevator.

"I believe you know your way from here," Albert said. "By the way, Mister

Van Loan, that is an elegant tuxedo."

Van grinned at the compliment. "Just another uniform, Albert." He stepped into the car and the doors slid shut behind him. Only two buttons on the panel, Up and Down. That's how you know you've got it made, Van thought. No need to bother with anything in between. The elevator rose smoothly to the top of the building. The doors opened with a pneumatic hiss and Van stepped into the foyer of Frank's suite.

A single banker's lamp on an unoccupied desk was the only light in the room. Frank's secretary Doris had left hours before. Van crossed the room and knocked on the door to the publisher's inner sanctum.

In a moment, Frank Havens opened the door and motioned Van inside. He put a finger to his lips. He was in shirtsleeves and suspenders, his tie pulled down. Van could smell scotch on his breath.

Frank's office was more like a study in a wealthy man's mansion than a place of business. At one end of the room were comfortable leather armchairs, a fire in a rough stone hearth, and framed prints of Western scenes by Remington and Russell. At the other end sat Frank's desk, piled as always with papers, galleys in long strips spilling over the edges.

A man approximately Van's age sat in one of the chairs by the fire. He was dark haired and clean shaven. His suit must have cost half a year's salary for the average working stiff. His head turned toward Van and he cocked it as if he were listening for Van rather than looking for him, and Van realized he was blind. The man pulled back his sleeve and put his fingers on the face of a pricey watch that Van could see had had its crystal removed.

"That was quick," the blind man said.

"Clark," Havens said, "this is the man I told you about." He turned to Van. "This is Clark Spender."

That Frank didn't name him put Van immediately on his guard. "How do you do," he said, altering his voice to a lower pitch and a gruff tone.

"Not well, I'm afraid," Spender said, taking a cigarette case from his pocket. Before either Van or Frank could offer a light, Spender produced one of his own and flicked it to flame. He put his index finger at the tip of the cigarette and by feel brought the flame close enough to light it. "I came to Frank in the hope that he could help me solve two murders and prevent four others. He said perhaps the Phantom Detective could solve my dilemma."

Van shot a sharp look at Frank, who shrugged, palms up.

Frank waved Van to the armchairs. "Clark, why don't you tell him the story?"

Spender inhaled deeply. "Crime doesn't pay, but fighting it must. That's a pricey cologne, my friend. *Roué*, isn't it?"

Van said curtly, affecting his Phantom persona. "Okay, pal. You've proved yourself. Now tell me why we're here."

"When the War began, I was a student at Dartmouth. I belonged to the rich boys' fraternity, Zeta Lambda Mu. A gang of us, ten in all, formed a sort of inner clique. We called ourselves 'The Crew' and spent a lot of time drinking, sporting, and generally debauching. We knew we would all be drafted sooner or later, and one night after a long bout of drinking, we came up with an idea. Our current enthusiasm was Sherlock Holmes, and we decided that since we'd all be going to war, like the men in 'A Study in Scarlet' we should form a tontine. Familiar to you?"

"Yeah. A kind of insurance policy; an annuity shared by members of a common fund. As members kick off, the shares get bigger. The last survivor collects the whole works."

"Correct. We were all from well to do families, so it was no stretch for each of us to put in a hundred dollars. Myself, Sam Lonnigan, Wilson Masters, Robert Cavett, Gavin Marquest, Bart Mayhew, Colin Koch, Aaron Lindsey, Anson Willamette, and Lloyd Montrose.

"It all seemed a joke at the time. When you're twenty years old, you think you're invulnerable, but war is war. We all went, and remarkably, only three of us didn't come back. Gavin Marquest and Bart Mayhew were infantrymen and killed in combat. Bob Cavett was an airman. He was shot down over France. Seven of us returned. Some of us," he raised his hand to his eyes, "came back damaged in one way or another.

"Colin's father, Alvin Koch, was one of the Wizards of Wall Street. You're familiar with the name?"

"I've heard of him."

"We agreed that we would turn the tontine money over to him to invest and make the pot bigger. Alvin Koch invested the tontine money wisely, and it grew to a tidy sum, over twenty-five thousand dollars in the next ten years."

"And the Crash of Twenty-Nine didn't wipe it out?"

Spender shook his head. "Koch was one of the smart insiders who sold short. Our investment was protected. Since the market recovered, it's grown even more. Nearly forty thousand dollars now."

"Two months ago, Aaron Lindsey's wife came home to find him dead in his car. The police called it a suicide; garage door closed, engine running. But there was no note. Then just two weeks ago, Lloyd Montrose was shot and killed when he surprised a burglar, or so the police said. No witnesses, no clues."

Van pondered this for a moment. "And you think one of The Crew is murdering the others to collect on the tontine?"

"I think it's a good possibility."

"It could all be coincidence."

"Not all of us are living as well as I am. The Depression makes forty thousand dollars worth killing for to a lot of people."

"And the police?"

"Lindsey lived in Connecticut; Montrose in Jersey. Different police departments, jurisdictional issues, not enough for the FBI, so Frank suggested I talk with you."

Van turned to Frank. "I had misgivings about involving you in a matter like this one, but Clark's late father was a good friend of mine. And, murder is murder. If anyone could crack the case, it would be the Phantom Detective."

"So, Spender, you've been in touch with the survivors?"

Spender nodded. "I have more time on my hands than most people, and more money. I employ a clipping service to keep tabs on my friends. Two dead in six weeks seemed more than coincidental."

Van was silent a moment. "I'll think about it. I'd need a list of the tontine members, dead or alive, any information you can give me about them."

Spender's hand dipped into a valise beside his chair. He ran his finger over the tab of a thick file folder and held it out to Van. "All here."

"You were pretty confident that I'd get involved," Van growled.

"Let's say I had faith that the Phantom Detective couldn't refuse the challenge."

"One question, Spender: why not hire a private eye or the Pinkertons? You can obviously afford either or both."

"I want to stay alive. I wanted the best, and someone who isn't hampered by the rulebook. And as you observed, money is no object."

"I don't work for money."

"That's what Frank told me. But I will front any expenses." He reached into his briefcase again and drew out a banded stack of hundred dollar bills, which he set on the coffee table.

Van let it lie. "Frank will be in touch." Without another word, Van stood and left the office. As he rode the elevator to the lobby, he turned the details over in his mind. Forty grand was more than enough to inspire a murderer. Hell, it was still the Depression. There were people on the street who'd kill you for a five dollar bill. The problem with the cops has always been that they are reactive not proactive. Their job is to solve crime, not so much so to prevent it.

He could pursue the investigation under the guise of writing a feature article for the Clarion and using that pretense, he could gather the information he needed. Once he had a solid picture of the situation, he could plan a course of action to see that the murderer, if there was one, would not murder again.

• • •

Spender sipped his scotch."Well, what do you think?"

Frank ran his hand through his wiry gray hair. "He didn't say no."

"He didn't say yes, either. Maybe he thinks because we're Ivy Leaguers we're not worth his time."

Frank shrugged, then remembered that it was a useless gesture. He didn't dare say the Phantom was a rich man too, or anything that would give even a hint at his identity. "The word I'd use to describe him is 'egalitarian.' Crime is crime, and he's devoted to fighting it."

"Let's hope he succeeds while you're still breathing."

• • •

As Rodney drove him to his apartment, Van ran his thumb over the blank tab of the manila folder Spender had given him. Not exactly blank; Van could feel the raised bumps of Braille characters. Another little stunt of Spender's to teach a lesson to the sighted: You can read a printed page and I can't, but I can read Braille and you can't.

Spender didn't know that The Phantom had learned to read Braille years before when he cracked the case of Willem McMonigle's murder by mobsters. McMonigle wrote article after article exposing Mob ties to politicians and had acid thrown in his face, blinding him for his trouble. McMonigle continued his quest and the Mob followed up with a hail of machine gun fire on a Manhattan sidewalk outside his apartment building.

The Braille bumps read: The Tontine Ten.

"Hot story, Van?" Rodney said.

"Maybe. Frank wants me to look into it." Van didn't elaborate, and Rodney didn't pursue it. Feature writing for the Clarion was an effective cover for Van's investigative research. It allowed him unquestioned access to the Clarion's morgue and usually unchallenged inquiries in other places. Other reporters and editors regarded him as a rich-boy dilettante, but his stories held their own with the best in the City.

Rodney pulled the Dusenberg to the curb in front of the Park Avenue high rise. Van opened the door and stepped onto the sidewalk. "That'll be it for tonight, Rod. I'll see you in the morning."

"Yes, sir." Rodney touched a two finger salute to the brim of his cap and the Dusenberg rolled silently away.

Van stood outside for a moment looking up one side of the street and then the other. The opulent neighborhood stretched to a vanishing point. The wealth of the nation was quartered here, and he was a part of it. But the life of the indolent rich held no attraction for Van. As a pilot in the War, he learned that his motivation was adventure, danger, the adrenaline rush of conflict, not the accumulation of more wealth than he had already inherited. Spender had struck the right nerve; the challenge of preventing murder rather than solving it was irresistible.

"Good evening, Mister Van Loan." The doorman affected the same salute as Rodney's.

"Good evening, Ralph."

The liveried doorman looked almost cartoonish in his red jacket with its gold braid and epaulettes, but under the coat were a .45 automatic and a sap. No one would invade this palace of the rich unscathed. Van stepped into his private elevator and in a moment arrived at the foyer of his penthouse.

Inside, he went into the study, poured himself three fingers of rye and hung his jacket over the back of his desk chair. The room was lined with book cases floor to ceiling on two walls. A fireplace and mantel occupied a third wall and a bay window overlooking the skyline the fourth. An original Gaugin of a bare breasted Tahitian woman drawing water hung over the fireplace, and a pair of Tiffany lamps flanked his comfortable leather reading chair.

He untied the string on the file. Van half expected it to be in Braille like the tab, but even Spender wasn't that coy. Included with a thick sheaf of press clippings were typewritten sheets, page after page of onion skin paper. It would be a long night. He dropped into the chair and began to read.

An hour later, a telephone bell. Van opened a lower drawer of his desk and pulled out a bulky Stromberg handset. "Is he gone, Frank?" Only Havens had the private number.

"Spender? Yeah. He left a while ago." Silence for a minute. "What do you think, Van?"

"I think I was ambushed."

"Spender's a cocky bastard, but I owe his father— big time."

"You knew I'd take the case."

"You can't pass up a challenge, Van. Never could."

"Now who's being cocky?"

"If I'd told you ahead of time, would it have made a difference?"

"Maybe. Maybe not."

"So what do I tell Clark?"

"Nothing. Let him sweat a day. It'll do his sense of entitlement some good."

Frank chuckled at the other end of the line. "Right. What do I do with the cash he left?"

"I'll think about it. Put it in your safe for now."

"I suggested they break up the tontine; divvy up the forty grand six ways and make the take less attractive."

"Good evening, Mr. Van Loan."

"Nobody in his right mind would kill the others so he could get the money. He'd be the most obvious suspect. There has to be more to it than the cash."

"My thinking too, Van. And if anyone can savvy it out it's you."

"Thanks for your vote of confidence. I have a lot of reading to do, Frank. Goodnight."

Van hung up the phone and closed the drawer. More to it. A lot more to it. Time to go to work.

• • •

For all his annoying smugness, Spender had done as good a job as anyone could assembling information about the tontine subscribers. Little more than obits for the three war casualties, and simple profiles of the men who survived the war but were barely surviving the Depression. They were the most obvious suspects, but Van had to consider the others as thoroughly. Van's lifelong association with the world's wealthy had taught him a simple truth: for some people, there can never be enough money. The final document was a photostat copy of the tontine, a handwritten page with the drunken scrawl of ten signatures. Betting against death and, ironic, perhaps inviting it.

Van started with the smallest dossiers. There was little on the three deceased members of the Crew. Gavin Marquest's and Bart Mayhew's obituaries were the end of their respective stories. Marquest was buried in France with members of his unit, but Mayhew, whose father was a Washington bigwig, had his body shipped back to the States to occupy a plot in Arlington. Lieutenant Robert Cavett's story didn't even get that far. His body was never recovered and his biplane never found.

Aaron Lindsey inherited his father's insurance business, one of the most successful in Connecticut, but when the Depression hit, the average Joe saw buying insurance of any kind a form of locking the barn door after the fact. His sales fell, and his once prosperous business withered. Lindsey was on the verge of bankruptcy; he had let employees go one after another until he practically ran the business alone. Police attributed his death to despondency over his failure. It was too common an event to dismiss as a theory.

Lloyd Montrose was another story. He came back from the War to enter the rough and tumble world of the speculator. When the crash came in twenty-nine, he lost it all but through hard work and cutthroat business practices, he fought his way back. He was well on his way to his first million when a burglar's bullet put him down. Based on some of the articles in his file, Montrose was as hated as anyone on Wall Street, and there was talk in some circles that it was no burglar, but rather someone Montrose ruined who pulled the trigger.

Then came the living; suspects as well as potential victims. There was little more information on Wilson Masters than those killed in the War. A victim of chemical warfare, mustard gas, Masters spent the first years after his return in and out of hospitals to treat his damaged lungs. He was living with a sister in Ossining and working as a bookkeeper for a trucking company.

He had no pension from the Army. One of the most shameful examples of the abuse of veterans in Van's eyes was the 1924 law that granted bonuses to World War I veterans in the form of certificates they could not redeem until 1945, by which time many of them would be dead.

Anson Willamette was a little better off. He worked as a clerk in a hardware store in Newark. The job didn't pay much but between that and an allowance from his aging father, he was able to keep his head above water. A shoulder injury kept him from manual labor, and he was fortunate to have a job at all.

Sam Lonnigan was the most elusive. Following the War, he simply dropped out of sight. Spender's people eventually traced him to a railway company, for whom an educated man worked as a gandydancer, swinging a sledgehammer by day and drinking away his wages by night. He was one whom the Depression seemed to affect the least. He drifted from job to job, his drunkenness condemning him to life at hard labor. At the time of the murders, he was working as a laborer on the Triborough Bridge.

Any of those three would find the tontine money a temptation, Van thought. And all three were within easy traveling distance of the murder sites.

Then there was Colin Koch. A wealthy playboy, he inherited more money than he could spend in his lifetime from his father, who made sure that the scion of the Koch family rode a desk for the duration of the War. Of the remaining members of the Crew, he seemed to be the least likely to murder for money.

And as foolish as it seemed, he had to consider Clark Spender a suspect. A blind man could still pull a trigger or drop a mickey into someone's highball and put his unconscious body behind the wheel of an idling automobile. Maybe he had an accomplice. Some of the other survivors had disabilities, but who among them was more disabled than Spender?

But if it were Spender, why call attention to the case and bring in the Phantom? Van recalled the almost boastful way Spender showed off his independence and capability. Maybe he wanted a challenge too, to match wits with the best criminal mind in New York.

Van shook his head. He favored Ockham's Razor over pretzel logic. The simplest solution to a problem is most likely the correct one. But instinct told him to keep Clark Spender on the list.

Havens' idea of breaking up the tontine and splitting the dough was a good one. The file included a photographic copy of the tontine agreement. Reading it told Van that dissolution would require unanimous agreement among the survivors. The prospect might bring the asp from under the proverbial rock. It would best be done with all of them assembled, and in a circumstance in which the Phantom could be present to observe and respond.

Van opened his desk drawer and dialed Frank Havens' number. He answered on the fourth ring. "Havens."

"You know who this is," Van said in a gruff voice.

"Yeah. I do."

"Tomorrow, call Spender and here's what I want you to tell him…."

• • •

The train rolled further from the concrete and steel of New York City and deeper into the forests at the center of the state. The further the train went, the towns got smaller and the trees got taller until the birch, beech and maple trees that lined either side of the tracks. The Phantom sat by the window of the Pullman coach with a book in his lap. He favored detective stories because despite their outlandish plots, they often provided insight into a new motive or a new method, usually of murder.

But at the moment, his attention was focused on a group of three men seated face to face a few rows forward and what snatches of their conversation he could hear over the rattling of the wheels. The Phantom recognized Sam Lonnigan, Wilson Masters, and Anson Willamette from photographs Clark Spender had provided. Spender was correct when he said that not all of the Tontine Ten were as prosperous as he. All three wore new suits, provided by Spender along with the rail tickets.

Lonnigan's face, under his snap brim cap, was weathered from hard outdoor work, his bulbous nose peeling from sunburn. Gin blossoms spread across his cheeks. His rawboned frame stretched the shoulders of his jacket. Masters looked pale and almost cadaverous, a haunted look in his dark eyes. Of the three, he was the only one not smoking, and he seemed to shrink away from the smoke of Lonnigan's cigarette and Willamette's pipe. Mustard gas, thought the Phantom, chronic bronchitis and pulmonary edema. Willamette seemed the best off of the three, relatively speaking; the softness of his features and his pudgy build told the Phantom that he was at least well fed.

The snatches of their conversation that the Phantom heard over the clatter of the rails was largely mundane for the first hour or so; where they had gone after the War and where they had gone after the crash of twenty-nine, stories of hard luck and hard work, and stories of survival. The conversation drifted to nostalgic reminiscence; the halcyon days at Dartmouth, nights of carousing that Dionysus would envy, and romantic adventures that would make Don Juan blush.

Finally, after dancing around the subject as long as they could, Willamette said, "Hell of a thing about Lindsey and Montrose. Do you think Spender's right? Somebody wants to murder us all for the tontine money?"

Masters coughed wetly into a handkerchief, studied it a moment, then shoved it back into his pocket. "He'd better hurry up if he wants to include me."

"I suppose it's possible," Lonnigan said. "Forty grand is a lot of dough. Spender doesn't need it, and neither does Koch. So that leaves the three of us."

"It sure as hell isn't me," Masters said. "I probably won't live long enough to spend it."

"I'm not prosperous by any stretch," said Willamette, "but I'm not stupid or crazy enough to pull a stunt like this. The last man standing would be the first man the police would go after."

"I guess that leaves me," Lonnigan said with a bitter laugh, "on my way to the hangman. I'd forgotten all about the damned tontine until Spender contacted me. It's weird that Spender's kept tabs on all of us since the War."

"But he never contacted me all this time," Masters said. "Did he contact any of you?"

Heads shook.

"A rich man's hobby," Lonnigan said, lighting another cigarette. "Well, I have news for the killer, if there is one." He pulled aside his coat to reveal a revolver in his waistband. "If he tries for me, I won't go easy. I killed a lot of men in the Argonne who were trying to kill me. One more won't matter."

The train began to slow and the conductor walked through droning. "Birch Springs. This stop is Birch Springs."

As the train rumbled to a stop, the men rose. Willamette pulled a suitcase from the overhead rack. Neither Lonnigan or Masters had one. The Phantom waited until they left the car to pull his valise from beneath his seat. Taking the train had given him some insight, but the next twelve hours would be crucial. He pulled his mirrored cigarette case from his pocket and checked his makeup. Graying mustache, heavy brows, and fine lines at the corners of his mouth and eyes, adding fifteen years to his appearance and concealing his features.

He stood and strode slowly to the car's exit, walking with a practiced limp leaning on a cane with an ivory knob at its head. Besides being an effective bludgeon, a twist of the knob would fire a .410 shotgun shell from the tip. The conductor offered him a hand stepping from the car to the platform, which he accepted, and the Phantom found himself in the middle of nowhere. On the other side of the tracks, he saw nothing but pine trees, east or west.

At the end of the platform, the Phantom saw a bearded man in chauffeur's livery talking with his fellow passengers. The chauffeur turned and saw him and called out. "Mister Baines?"

"Yes, I'm Robert Baines."

"I'm Laszlo, Mister Koch's driver. I'm to take all of you to the Lodge." The Phantom placed his accent as Hungarian or perhaps Czech. The Phantom limped down the platform and Laszlo met him halfway, taking his valise. "This way, sir." As he passed the survivors, he said, "Come with me, gentlemen." He led them to an Oldsmobile sedan parked behind the station. The Phantom could see a few buildings a hundred yards down the road, no doubt Birch Springs' general store, post office, and local church.

Laszlo opened the front passenger door for the Phantom, and Lonnigan, Masters and Willamette climbed into the back seat. Laszlo got in and stepped on the starter. The engine turned a few revolutions and then he switched on the ignition. The Oldsmobile's engine purred into life.

"Sounds as if you need to set your timing," Lonnigan said from the back seat.

"No, sir. The oil settles into the crankcase when the engine is idle. Turning it over a few times first moves oil into the cylinders. It is good for the engine."

As Laszlo drove them through the dense forest, the Phantom stole a side-wise glance at the Chauffeur. His heavy black beard covered masses of thick scar tissue that crept out past its edges. His right eye was pulled downward slightly by the proud flesh, but seemed to function normally. Heavy scarring on his right hand had fused his ring and little fingers into a single wrinkled digit.

The Phantom noted the bulge in Laszlo's right armpit. Either Koch's chauffeur doubled as his bodyguard or had been armed for the occasion. It also told him that Laszlo was left handed, sinister as opposed to Dexter, perhaps because of his injury.

The big sedan rolled through corridors of the birch trees that gave the hamlet its name. The road was rutted by the passage of logging trucks, but the Oldsmobile gave a much smoother ride than the Phantom would have imagined.

"If you don't mind me asking," Masters said from the back seat, "who might you be?"

"My name is Robert Baines." The Phantom pulled a business card from his vest and handed it over the seat. "Attorney-at-Law."

The survivors passed the card among them each examining it in turn.

"I've been engaged by Mister Spender."

"Is that so? An attorney, eh?" Lonnigan said.

What little conversation that had passed among them suddenly ceased, as if on an unseen signal, and the car was quiet for the rest of the drive. The only break in the monotony of the trees was a small lake that came almost to the edge of the road.

"Are there fish in the lake?" the Phantom asked.

"Yes, sir," Laszlo replied. "It's part of Mister Koch's property. He keeps it stocked with trout and bass."

The Oldsmobile rounded a bend and drove through an archway with a double leaved wrought iron gate. At the top of the arch were the words The Beeches. The Phantom glanced at his watch. Seventeen minutes at moderate speed. The driveway was at least fifty yards long and wound through the trees in graceful esses. It was gravel that popped and crunched under the tires as the car rolled up to the house.

To call it a house understated the case tenfold. The Beeches was more like a small hotel, a three story rough stone edifice that rose to the tops of the trees that closed around it like a stockade. A broad veranda spanned the front of the building and wrapped around its left side. A balcony spanned the second floor and French windows gave the rooms access. The roof was dark gray slate tinted with the green of moss. All in all, an imposing building.

Laszlo parked the car at the broad front steps and opened the doors for his passengers. "I will take your bags, gentlemen."

The Phantom climbed the steps deliberately, leaning on his cane.

"The War?" Willamette said as he passed him on the steps.

The Phantom nodded. "Took a round in my knee. Hurts like the devil when it's going to rain."

"So does my shoulder, but not from a bullet. A bunker collapsed when a grenade exploded. Caved in on me. Six inches to the right, and it would have crushed my skull."

"Sherman had it right."

"How's that?"

"War is hell."

Laszlo opened the front door, itself a slab of solid oak stained almost black and fitted with heavy strap hinges. It gave onto a broad foyer with a staircase opposite the doorway. Descending it were Clark Spender and another man whom the Phantom recognized as Colin Koch. Spender was dressed as he was at Havens' office. Koch wore khaki trousers and a green plaid Pendleton shirt over a white turtle-necked sweater.

Everything in the foyer spoke of money, but its effect seemed false, as if it were some interior decorator's version of how a hunting lodge should look. The result gave the Phantom the impression that any second someone would yell,

"Cut!" everyone would relax their poses, and a director in a beret and jodhpurs would bark orders through a megaphone.

There was silence for a moment, and Koch said, "Anson, Sam, Wilson, good that you're all here." The remark fell flat. Masters gave a thick, wet cough. The pair descended the stairs and Lonnigan said, "Looks as if some of us have done all right."

"There but for fortune," Koch replied with a thin smile and a shrug.

"Yeah, your old man's fortune." If Willamette's remark was intended to offend, it had the opposite effect. The tension broken, everyone burst into laughter.

"Same old Annie," Koch said. "Quickest wit in Dartmouth." He crossed the foyer to shake hands with his guests. Spender followed close behind with a hand on Koch's shoulder. As they all shook hands, the Phantom noticed their little fingers separated from the rest to go tip to tip to form a triangle. Part of the Zeta Lambda Mu identification ritual; the triangle was really the Greek letter Delta, standing for Dedication.

As Spender shook hands with each, he lingered for a few seconds, gathering as much as his senses would allow; the timbre of a voice, the scent of a specific tobacco, the feel of a callused or a smooth palm, all filed away for future reference.

"And this is my attorney, Robert Baines, Colin."

"Pleased," Koch said. His grip was strong and his manner confident. "I say what we all need is a good stiff drink. Follow me." As Koch led the group past the staircase, he said over his shoulder, "Laszlo, please take the gentlemen's bags to their rooms."

The den was, like the foyer, the image of what a den in a rustic lodge should be. A fireplace of the same stone as the lodge's exterior, trophy heads of bear, deer, and elk. Sofas and chairs with frames of rough hewn wood and cushions upholstered in plaid burlap. A baby grand piano dominated one corner of the room, and a rack of bookshelves another. It was a room designed to relax.

Spender sat on one of the sofas and fingered a native blanket thrown over the back. "Navajo. I can tell by the weave. Colin, you should have Oneida or maybe Mohawk to be anthropologically accurate."

Koch laughed. "Talk to my decorator." He strode to a well stocked wet bar. "What'll you all have?" He held up a crystal decanter. "Kentucky bourbon aged in the cask. Join me?

There was agreement all around except for Spender, who said, "Surprise me."

Koch reached under the counter of the bar and pulled out a dark bottle. He poured two fingers and placed the tumbler in Spender's hand. Spender swirled the amber liquid in the glass and inhaled its aroma like a wine steward. He took a sip sloshed it around his tongue, and smiled. "*Eau-d- vie.* French brandy. Raynal, I think."

"Raynal and Cie," Koch said.

"Excellent." Spender inhaled the fume. "But it should be in a snifter. You put it in a highball glass to fool me."

"There's no fooling you, Clark."

The Phantom sat beside Spender and said quietly below the chatter, "Have I seen everyone now?"

Spender replied, "All but Luke, my chauffeur. I sent him into town for a few things. He should be back any time."

"I think a toast is in order." Koch raised his glass. "To brothers; brothers in Zeta Lambda Mu, brothers in arms, and brothers lost and living."

"Hear, hear!" said Willamette.

The toast was drunk, and after a moment's reflection, Willamette said, "This 'Hail fellow' stuff is all well and good, but that's not why we're here. If you cared a bit about us, you'd've called The Crew together years ago. But now it seems your neck's on the line with the rest of us. So what about this business with the tontine and Lindsey and Montrose?"

If Koch was offended by the remark or Willamette's tone, it didn't show.

"Don't be so uncharitable, Anson." Spender turned his sightless eyes toward him. "We may all be in danger— all but one of us, or we may not. I prefer to err on the side of caution if that's the case."

Koch looked at the cathedral clock on the mantel. "It's nearly seven. Mrs. Gabler, the cook prepared supper before she left for the evening. I'm sure we're all hungry. Let's put pleasure before business, just like the old days, and enjoy supper. Then we can talk."

As they walked of the den, the Phantom saw Lonnigan open the onyx cigarette box on the coffee table and scoop out a handful, which he shoved into his pocket. He had also poured himself another whiskey from the crystal decanter on the bar. Lonnigan looked up. He saw the Phantom watching him and his face became a deeper shade of red.

The Phantom shrugged and moved on, deciding that he couldn't chastise Lonnigan for his behavior any more than he might a dog who takes a steak from the dinner table when his back was turned. Circumstance had made him that way. The question was, to what extent.

Supper was laid family style at the long kitchen table. "So that no one is worried about having his plate laced with poison, we'll all serve ourselves from a common bowl," Koch said. "If you want to wait until I've had a few bites, I understand." He ladled a generous portion of the rich stew onto his plate and took a forkful while the others watched then everyone else dug in.

"Don't be so uncharitable, Anson."

The stew was delicious, and Mrs. Gabler's fresh baked cherry pie was probably the tastiest the Phantom had ever eaten. All agreed to not discuss the tontine during supper, and the conversation drifted through FDR's New Deal, the recovering economy, and finally settled on the rise of fascism in post war Germany.

"Hitler's rearming Germany in spite of Versailles," Willamette said.

"And he's building an air force," Koch added. "I doubt he has peaceful intentions."

"'The war to end all wars,'" Masters snorted. "I knew we'd be fighting in Europe again before too long."

"What do you think, Baines?" Spender said. "You've been quiet all evening."

"I listen and learn," the Phantom said. "I see Adolph Hitler as the threat. Germany will follow his lead because he promises a restoration of national pride. Germany was humiliated by the War, and Hitler is making his followers proud to be Germans again. I see him as an evil genius, and one who may plunge Europe into war very soon."

"We crushed the Krauts then, and we'll crush 'em again," Lonnigan said, his speech slurred by the whiskey. "I never met a German worth anything. Waste of blood and bone, I say."

"I'll vote for that," Masters said with a cough. "The soulless bastards gassed us in the trenches like we were so many rats."

"That won't happen again," said Spender. "The Treaty of Verasilles—"

"Treaties," Lonnigan snorted. "Worthless pieces of paper. Hitler's got that treaty hanging in his outhouse, I'd say."

Koch rose. "Gentlemen, let's retire to the den." Lightning flashed in the window behind him, and in its white glare, the Phantom saw a figure outside. His hand slid under his coat for the automatic tucked in his waistband. In seconds, there was a knock at the pantry door.

"Laszlo," Koch called, "see who that is."

"Probably Luke," Spender said. It turned out he was right. The chauffeur came in carrying a few parcels tied with string. He was a young man, fresh faced and clean shaven but for a thin mustache. He was dressed in an ordinary suit and necktie. Apparently Spender put little stock in appearances.

"Looks like a pretty nasty storm is brewing." He set the packages on the counter. To Spender, he said, "That general store is pretty well stocked. I found everything you asked for."

"Cabot's Store serves a dozen logging operations in a twenty mile radius," Koch explained. "They pretty much have one of everything."

"Gentlemen, this is Luke, my driver." His head swiveled to the chauffeur. "Please take those things up to my room and come back down for some of this delicious stew."

"Yes, sir."

"Now, as I was saying, let's go to the den. Brandy, cigars, and a long talk."

The group left the table and headed for the den. Lonnigan led the way, anxious to get to the whiskey. He was pouring a stiff drink from the decanter when the Phantom entered.

"This is good stuff," Lonnigan said to Koch, He took a long swallow.

"It ought to be. It's eighty years old and costs two hundred a bottle."

Lonnigan grinned. "Now that's—" His face went blank and his eyes darted around the room as if looking for an answer to what was happening to him. The others stood frozen in shock as he dropped his on the carpet and clutched at his throat with both hands. He began to weave on his feet as flecks of foam oozed from the corners of his mouth.

Lonnigan pitched forward, grabbing at the back of a chair which he pulled over with him, and crashed to the floor. His body quivered, and he lay still.

"My God," someone said.

The men stood in stunned silence staring at Lonnigan.

"What's happening?" Spender said. "What's going on?"

"It looks as if you are right," Koch said. "Lonnigan is dead." He turned to the doorway. "Laszlo! Lazslo! Get in here!"

In seconds, the chauffeur dashed into the room. "Yes, Mister Koch. I— " He stared at the dead man on the floor and crossed himself.

"Where's your man Luke?" Koch said.

"He is in the kitchen eating his supper," Laszlo answered. "Shall I get him?"

"Yes," Koch said. "Bring him now."

"So," Willamette said, "There is a killer among us."

"But we all drank from that decanter earlier," said Masters. "Except him." He pointed an accusing finger at Spender. "He drank something different."

"Which could have just as easily been poisoned as the decanter, Wilson." Spender shot back. "You all drank from it, and you're still alive. Someone poisoned the whiskey while we were eating supper."

"Yes," the Phantom said, "I saw Lonnigan pour himself a drink from it as the rest of you were leaving the room, and he didn't keel over dead then."

Masters leapt at the body and rolled it over, grabbing the revolver from Lonnigan's waistband. He rose into a crouch, aiming it in a wide sweep. "All of you, get back. I may not live much longer but I'm not going to die tonight."

"Come on, Wilson," Koch said. "Be sensible. Put it down."

"Be sensible? That's what people say when I won't do what they want me to do. Oh no, I am being sensible. I'm getting out of here. I—" His words devolved into a coughing fit that racked his body.

A blur from the doorway. Laszlo threw himself into Masters, knocking him sideways, and wrestled the gun from him. "Sir?" Laszlo looked to Koch for direction, aiming the pistol at Masters' head.

Koch raised his hands in a restraining gesture. "No. Let's get him up." Willamette and Koch took Masters by the elbows and set him in an easy chair. Masters' breath was wet and ragged. Without warning, he coughed violently, spraying his shirt and necktie with bloody froth."Take him to his room and lay him on the bed. Give me the pistol." Laszlo handed Koch the gun.

"Luke, help him."

Luke took Masters' feet and Laszlo his shoulders. They carried him out of the room and up the staircase.

"We need a doctor," said Willlamette.

"And the police," the Phantom said. "There's been a murder here and we're all suspects."

"Speak for yourself," Willamette said. "I didn't kill anybody. I was nowhere near that decanter. My money's on Masters. He killed the man with the gun and was ready to run out the door and escape."

"To what end?" Spender said. "To kill Lonnigan in front of us all then run would make him the prime suspect. He'd never get away with it. And besides, if he were the killer, he could have just shot us like tin cans on a fence."

Koch said, "I'll call the police and an ambulance."

Spender shook his head. "A doctor, yes. An ambulance, no."

"What?"

"Colin, an ambulance will take Masters away. Keep in mind why we're all here. Tell them, Baines."

The Phantom cleared his throat. "The purpose of this meeting is to discuss the revocation of the tontine, removing the incentive for the killer to murder the other survivors. The tontine requires unanimous consent for its dissolution. Take Masters away, and it stands as written and three of you are still targets."

"So, Colin, call a doctor," Spender said, "and the police."

"Not police; the Sheriff." Koch nodded and left the room.

"I want to know something, Spender," Willamette said, an edge in his voice. "How did you know your man Luke was in the room. You couldn't see him."

Spender turned to directly face him. "I know his step. I know his scent. Just as I know yours. My sight is gone, but I've trained my other senses to compensate."

"You're pretty confident for a blind man. I think you can see better than you let on."

"Is that so?" Spender pulled out a pocket automatic. "If you think my blindness ," he brushed his hands across his eyes, "is some sort of ruse— someone tie this around my eyes." He pulled a handkerchief from his pocket.

The Phantom obliged.

"Now," said Spender, "set a tumbler on the bar and everyone but you step away." Willamette did as instructed, and Spender said, "Drop a coin into it and step back."

Willamette threw a coin into the glass. It landed with a tinny clink. Spender swung the pistol. There was a sharp crack and the tinkle of glass shards on the bar and the floor.

"Holy Moses," said Willamette.

"When I lost my sight, I determined that I wouldn't let it hamper me. I've been trained by the best from the West and the Orient. I don't intend to allow some lunatic to kill me for forty thousand dollars any more than you do."

"Someone killed Lonnigan," the Phantom said, "but which one of us?"

"You said you saw Lonnigan pour himself a drink as we all left the den," Willamette said. "You were the last to the table. Maybe you did it, Baines."

"That's absurd," Spender shot back. "He'd have no reason to do such a thing."

"Unless he's working with you, Spender. Your eyes and maybe your hands."

"While we're looking at opportunity, how about my man Luke, or Laszlo? Maybe Luke is working for me, or Laszlo is working for Colin. But why would we kill? We don't need the money. You do, which brings suspicion back around to you, Anson."

Koch returned. "The Sheriff is coming now, and so is Doctor Branson from the village."

"Good. Now," said Spender. "While we wait, let's discuss the damned tontine and how we can extricate ourselves from it. Baines?"

The Phantom pulled a pair of rimless spectacles from his breast pocket and perched them on his nose. "The original agreement is pretty straightforward. The cumulative value of the tontine will go to the last subscribing survivor following the death of the others, if I may be redundant." He turned to the second page. "This is the sticking point: 'In order to dissolve this agreement, all parties hereto must agree unanimously.'"

"It's that good old Zeta Lambda Mu 'one for all and all for one' philosophy," Koch said.

"Yes," Spender agreed. "I say we end it and split the take. What do the rest of you think?"

"I say we end it and give half to Wilson and half to Annie. I'll forego my share."

"That suits me, Colin," Spender said. "I'll forfeit mine as well. Anson?"

"That's more than generous," he said.

"Well, hell, we don't need it as much as you do."

"Masters said something about using his share to go to a clinic in Arizona to treat his lungs," Willamette said. "Maybe that will help him."

"And will it satisfy you sufficiently to let the rest of us live?" Spender said.

Willamette's face reddened. "The devil you say. I'm needy but not desperate. If you give me two shares instead of four, I have no complaint. But once this business is done, I'm getting out of here."

Luke and Laszlo returned. "We put Mister Masters in his bed. He's sleeping for the moment."

Spender said, "Colin, I'm armed. Laszlo, give me the gun you took from Masters." Laszlo handed the revolver to him. "Anson, take it." He held out the gun butt first to Willamette, who tucked it into the waistband of his trousers. Spender swiveled his head toward Koch. "Colin, I assume you have guns here. Do you have enough pistols for yourself, Baines, Luke and Laszlo?"

"Of course." Koch turned to Laszlo. "You know where the key to the gun closet is. Bring three pistols."

"Only three?" Willamette said.

"Laszlo is already armed. Show them."

Laszlo pulled back his tunic to reveal the handle of a Colt automatic. "I'll go right now, sir."

"If we're going to revoke the tontine, we need Masters awake and aware," Willamette said.

"Or dead," the Phantom added. "One less required signature."

"Spoken like a true lawyer," Koch said.

"Only being pragmatic. We have a purpose to fulfill, and I am here to see it done. After all, I'm at as much risk as any of you. I'm here to make sure all is legal to avoid entanglements later. I want to conduct this business as quickly as possible. I'm already a witness to one murder, which makes me the killer's target too."

"I suppose that's true," Spender said. "But I don't think if we're all armed, the killer can get us all before one of us gets him."

"You're overlooking one thing," the Phantom said. "The killer may not be working alone. What if he's got a henchman hiding outside ready to pick us off through a window?"

Everyone but Spender turned to the French windows across the den. "Luke," Koch said, "Please draw the curtains."

Laszlo returned with a pocket sized automatic, a cowboy Colt .45, and a long barreled Remington target pistol. He offered them to the men. Luke took the Remington and Koch the Colt, leaving the automatic for the Phantom.

"Masters is alone upstairs," Willamette said. "Shouldn't he be down here with us? And what about a gun for him?"

Koch said, "I don't think he'll be in any shape to pull a trigger. Laszlo, keep an eye on him 'til the doctor arrives."

"Yes, sir."

"And now we wait." Koch gave a sardonic chuckle. "I'd offer you a drink, but—"

For several minutes the men sat in silence. Finally, Koch said, "I don't think the Sheriff will mind if we cover Lonnigan. I don't mind telling you it gives me the willies staring at his corpse."

The Phantom said, "This is a crime scene. We can't touch anything."

"Well, I'm going to touch that bottle of brandy," Koch said. "I need a drink, and the anyone else who wants to join me can—"

A sharp knock came at the front door. "Luke, please see who it is."

In a moment, a stout man in a yellow rain slicker came in, carrying a doctor's bag. Rain dripped from the slicker onto the carpet. "Rainin' like a bitch out there. I'll be surprised if there's a road left by morning." He looked around the room. "You all look healthy as horses. Where's the patient?" Then he looked down and saw Lonnigan lying near the bar. He started toward him and Koch held out a restraining hand.

"He's dead. The Sheriff's on his way. The man who needs attention is upstairs. Luke will take you."

"One minute," the Phantom said. "Doctor, would you open your bag, please."

Branson blinked. "I beg your pardon?"

"Is that necessary?" Koch said. "I've known Doctor Branson for years."

"We don't," the Phantom said. "Doctor, if you please."

Branson set his bag on the coffee table. "Help yourself."

"This is ridiculous," Koch said.

"There's been a murder here," Spender said. "If I could see, I'd want a look too."

In a moment, everyone was satisfied, and the doctor was on his way to tend to Masters.

No one spoke for a time. Spender sipped his brandy. Koch fussed with the fire in the hearth. Willamette paced, and the Phantom sat smoking a cigarette, allowing the smoke to mask his studious gaze on the others. Finally, Willamette broke the silence. "Now all we need is the Sheriff to make the game complete."

"Odd choice of words, that," Spender quipped. "Is that how you see it? A game?"

"Well, no, I—"

"It's already occurred to me," said the Phantom, "that the killer may not be down on his luck. He may not need the money at all. He may simply be obsessed with proving something."

All eyes in the room turned to Spender, whose mouth turned upward in a devilish grin. "Who are you working for, Baines?" He pointed a finger at the Phantom. "Bang." His finger moved in less than a second to each man in the room. "Bang. Bang. Bang." He chuckled "If I wanted to, I could have killed you all in one breath. I don't need to prove myself to the likes of you."

"Enough of this nonsense," Koch snapped. He turned to the Phantom. "Baines, do you have the document ready for everyone to sign? I say get this damned business over with."

The Phantom nodded. "I have it ready to sign. It's in my brief case."

"Then let's do it."

"Is Masters conscious?"

"I don't know. We'll have to wait on Doctor Branson's word."

"Then I will have that drink, Colin," Spender said.

As Koch poured the brandy, Doctor Branson came in the room, "The man needs to be in a hospital, but I don't think an ambulance could get through."

"You did," said Spender."

"The nearest hospital is in Grayson," Koch said. "The roads are bad enough on a dry day from the logging trucks. They'd be impassable tonight. Doctor?"

"I gave him a sedative he'll— "

"You what?" Willamette sputtered. "A sedative? We need him awake."

"Well, he won't be for at least eight hours."

"Dear God!"

"Oh, Anson, relax," Spender said.

"That does complicate things," the Phantom said, setting a manila file folder on the coffee table. "Without his vote, we can't proceed." He shook his head. "And now we can't even get his proxy."

"Well, that's just great!" Willamette said. "Can't you wake him up for a few minutes?"

"Certainly not."

The telephone rang in the hallway, and in a moment, Koch stepped out into the foyer to answer it and returned in a moment. "Doctor, the call is for you."

"Thank you." He left the room, glaring at Willamette as he went.

"Eight hours." Spender chuckled. "That takes us 'til breakfast. Should make for an interesting night."

Branson returned. "That was the Sheriff. There's been an accident in the village. I have to go. I'll get my bag. I'll leave medicine on the nightstand if he wakes up."

"Is he in any danger, Doctor?" the Phantom said.

Spender snickered.

"You mean will he live? Very likely. His condition is severe, but with proper treatment, he should have a few more birthdays." Branson pulled on his slicker. He cast a look at Lonnigan's corpse on the floor by the bar. "Too bad I'm not the coroner. I could have saved him a trip out here. You probably won't see him before tomorrow."

"Luke will see you out," Koch said.

Willamette waved his arms in agitation. "This is crazy. We're trapped in this house, one of us a wolf, and the rest of us sheep."

"Speak for yourself, Anson," Spender said. "It's obvious we aren't going to get this tontine matter settled tonight. So, do we each go to our rooms and wait with a gun pointed at the door for a visitor? Or do we stay in this room and stare at each other 'til dawn?"

"The Sheriff will be here soon," Koch said.

"I'm sure he'll have some ideas." Spender smiled grimly at no one in particular. "I'm for us staying here— in this room. Food can be brought in, and a pot of coffee to keep us awake. And if one of us makes a wrong move, the others can deal with him."

"What about Masters?"

"Our men can carry him down here. He'll be just as comfortable on the sofa as a bed. And he'll be much safer."

"I agree," the Phantom said. "Luke, you and Laszlo bring Mister Masters down here, would you please."

Luke gave a curt nod. "Yes, sir, immediately."

"I'm glad the phone's still working," Willamette said.

"Who are you going to call? Daniel Boone to come to the middle of nowhere in this storm?"

"Damn you, Spender, I don't give a damn that you're blind. I've had enough of your wisecracks." He took a menacing step toward the blind man, who raised his hand in a supplicating gesture. "Easy, Anson. Sorry." He raised his snifter. "Must be the brandy."

"Mister Koch! Mister Koch!" Luke shouted down the stairs. "Come quickly! It's Mister Masters!"

Everyone ran up the staircase to the second floor hallway where the Phantom saw Luke standing in an open doorway. "In here, quickly!"

In the room, Laszlo sprawled unconscious in a chair. Masters lay in the bed, covers pulled to his chin. Koch pulled the duvet away, revealing an inflated blood pressure cuff around Masters' throat.

"Jesus Christ."

"Is he dead?"

"*Luke, you and Laszlo bring Mister Masters down here.*"

Koch reached to undo the cuff, and the Phantom snapped, "Don't touch it. It's evidence." He put a hand on Masters' brow. "He hasn't been dead for long."

"Someone tell me what's going on." Spender stood in the doorway, the last to arrive.

"Masters is dead," Koch said.

"Well then," Spender quipped. "Let's go back downstairs and void the tontine before someone else dies."

"You cold bastard." Willamette lunged, hands out, at Spender, but Spender was ready. He caught Willamette's forearm and threw him over his hip, landing him flat on his back. Before Willamette could collect his wits, Spender was kneeling on his chest, his pistol under the man's chin.

"I should kill you right now."

Willamette's mouth gaped.

"Spender." The Phantom laid a hand on Spender's shoulder. "Let him up. Don't you see? The killer is trying to get us to do his work for him. Don't be a part of it."

A long moment passed while Spender thought it over, then he rolled off Willamette's chest and stood, but he didn't put away his gun. "Laszlo is here. I smell him. Is he dead too?"

"No. He was knocked out," the Phantom said, stooping beside Luke's chair. He picked up a coffee cup that lay on the floor and sniffed it. "Someone drugged him."

"The doctor?" Spender's brow creased. "That makes no sense. He's not part of the tontine. He has no stake in the game."

"Unless he was hired help," the Phantom said. He turned to Koch. "You were out of the room when you called Branson. We didn't hear the conversation. You could buy him off with your pocket change."

"That's absurd," Koch shot back. "You just made my case for me, Baines. I don't need the tontine money. The Sheriff will be here soon. He can sort it out."

"Will he? Maybe you didn't call him at all, Koch. And if the doctor is working with you, his story about the accident in the village may be a complete fabrication. As for the money, I don't think this is about the tontine anymore. I think we're dealing with a psychopath; a clever one, but a psychopath none theless."

"And I'm it?" Koch snorted. "What utter nonsense."

"That's it," Willamette said. "I'm leaving." He pulled the pistol from his waistband and aimed it at the room in general. Anyone who tries to stop me will be sorry. You!" He pointed the gun at Luke. "You're driving me." He reached under Luke's coat and took his pistol. "Let's go. And if any of you comes down those stairs before I'm gone, I'll shoot you."

"You're making a big mistake, Willamette." Baines said.

"You're the one making a mistake. If you're smart, you'll leave this nuthouse too."

He backed out the door, a gun in each hand and Luke followed him.

No one spoke until they heard the slamming of the front door.

"There's your psychopath," Koch said. "I'm calling the Sheriff. Again."

Koch went downstairs to the telephone.

"What do you think?" Spender said.

"I don't know. After this, all bets are off. It could be Willamette; it could be Koch."

"What should we do?"

"We'd better go downstairs. Make sure Koch makes that call. Or better yet, make it ourselves."

"What about Laszlo?"

The Phantom took the chauffeur's hand in his and dug his thumbnail into the flesh between the thumb and forefinger. No response. He raised Laszlo's eyelid. The eye was rolled back and showed mostly white. "Laszlo isn't going anywhere."

A motor roared into life outside. "There goes Willamette." Spender said.

Headlights played through the downstairs windows as Luke turned the car around. In a moment, it was gone.

"I'm calling the Sheriff's office," the Phantom said. He crossed the foyer and lifted the earpiece from the hook. He rattled it a few times, frowned, and tried again. "Dead." A flash of lightning lit the windows and thunder boomed immediately afterward. "The storm, I suppose."

"Unless the line was cut."

Koch came out. "It's dead. I just tried to call."

"That's inconvenient," said Spender. "I wanted to tell the Sheriff that Annie just stole my car and kidnapped my driver."

"I'm guessing they won't get far. It's raining harder. Branson will probably come slogging back here before too long because his car's up to the axles in mud." Another lightning flash and an immediate cannonade of thunder. "The storm's right on top of us. If he's the killer, he picked a bad time to escape."

"And if he's not, he chose a good one." The Phantom led the men into the den. The fire had burned down and Koch threw another log onto the grate and poked the ashes.

"And then there were two," Spender said.

"Why two?" Koch asked. "Anson is still alive. Or do you know something I don't? Is your man Luke killing him as we speak?"

Spender laughed. "What a roller coaster this has been. Everybody suspects everybody except the killer. I meant there are only two of us left here. Baines doesn't count. It has to be you, or it has to be me. Who's left? Baines?"

"You are crazy. Baines is right, a crazy killer who doesn't give a damn about the tontine money. Luke wasn't with us when the whiskey was poisoned, but that doesn't mean he wasn't here. He could have come back from town any time and been lurking outside waiting for his chance." Koch pulled the heavy Colt from his waist and thumbed back the hammer.

"And I think you're in on it too, Baines." Koch leveled the revolver at the Phantom's chest. "I'm no fool, Spender. When you said you were bringing a lawyer named Robert Baines, I had my people check on him. There is no lawyer named Baines registered with the New York Bar Association."

"Put the gun down, Koch," the Phantom said, taking a step toward him.

"No closer or I'll fire."

The Phantom took another step and Koch pulled the trigger.

The hammer clicked on an empty shell. "Wha—?"

"Your pistol is empty." Laszlo stood in the doorway, his automatic in his hand. "But mine isn't." The thick accent was gone.

Spender smiled. "Welcome home, Cavett."

Koch's mouth gaped. "Cavett?"

"Yes, home. 'To say I am Lazarus returned from the dead to tell you all and I shall tell you all.' Remember how Professor Jessup harped on that damned line?"

"So, you killed Masters and Lonnigan. And now you're going to kill us too?" the Phantom said. "You'll never collect the tontine money. Willamette is on his way to the village. He'll 'tell all.'"

"He and that driver of Spender's will never arrive. I cut the brake lines in the car. They'll end up in that pond at the sharp curve or wrapped around a tree."

"I should have known," the Phantom said, "when you turned the engine over a few rotations before starting it. You were an airman, right Cavett?"

"You have no idea what it was like. Shot down, on fire from spilled fuel, my face a ruin, and no chance of treatment because I had to hide from the Germans. It became infected and I had to cauterize it with a hot knife. I survived, living like a rat in burned out barns and bombed out cellars. I wandered around the forest, delirious, and I saw a campfire. I stumbled into the camp not caring if it was Germans or Americans. I was lucky. And then the war was over."

"Why didn't you come home?" Spender asked. "We would have helped you. I would have helped you."

"Come home? To what?" Laszlo sneered. "Scorn? Revulsion? What woman would even look at me? Your pity's even worse, Spender. I grew the beard to cover my scars, and developed the accent so that I could pass for an immigrant and come back to good old America once I had a plan."

"But to kill everyone for the tontine money?" Koch said, "You'll never get away with it."

"I don't think he really wants the tontine money," the Phantom said. "He has other things in mind."

Laszlo laughed. "You're pretty smart, mister lawyer— Baines or whatever your real name is. I can tell you because I'm going to kill you all anyway." He lifted his chin toward Koch. "How many times I watched you open the safe behind that painting," he pointed to a canvas of horses running across a sky full of billowing clouds, "with a pocket monocular and practiced until I could open it in my sleep. I saw what's in there. When Roosevelt grabbed all the gold, you didn't give yours up. How much is in there? Half a million?"

"Close," Koch replied.

"I'll be able to live well on it in Europe or South America for the rest of my days."

"Then why not just take it and go? Why kill everyone?"

"Because I hate every one of you who came home and went back to your lives. The dead ones, Marquest and Mayhew; I have nothing against them. What does the Bible say? 'In death he is acquitted of his sin.' But the rest of you.... "

"We all were drafted, Cavett," Spender said. "We all took the same chance. Look at me. I certainly can't look at you."

Cavett ignored him. "I was the one of the whole lot of you who didn't come from a rich family. I was always the red-haired stepchild of the lot. Oh, I knew how the lot of you snickered at me behind my back." Cavett turned toward Koch. "And you, condescending to loan me the money to buy into the tontine because you knew I didn't have it. You have no idea how that stung me, Koch."

"And you've been nursing this grudge against me, against all of us for fifteen years?"

The Phantom slowly closed his grip on the head of his cane.

"Sixteen. Sixteen years, four months and twenty days. And now it's time for a reckoning."

"I know your gun is empty, Koch, and yours too, Baines. But yours isn't, Spender. Take it out slowly and drop it on the floor and kick it away from you. And you two, clap your hands"

"What?"

"Do it. Or I'll gut shoot you both."

"It's to cover any sound he makes while I still have my pistol. Go ahead. Do what he says."

Koch and the Phantom both began clapping their hands. Cavett quietly stepped to one side as Spender pulled out his pistol, holding it between his thumb and forefinger and dropped it with a clatter on the hardwood floor. He kicked it across the polished oak to bang against the baseboard.

When Cavett turned his head, the Phantom swung his cane upward and twisted the head. Fire spat from the cane's tip, and buckshot peppered Cavett's shoulder. He reeled backward, dropping his gun. The Phantom was reaching for the automatic behind his back when there was a bright flash and a sharp crack of thunder. The lights went out.

Spender dove for his pistol, knowing by sound where it had gone. In the waning firelight, the Phantom saw Cavett run through the door into the darkness of the foyer.

Spender fired at the retreating footsteps but too late.

"Stay down," the Phantom warned. He grabbed the ice bucket, now mostly filled with water and threw it on the embers. "Stay here. I'll go after him."

"Like hell," Spender said. "I'm in my element."

The Phantom didn't argue. He crept into the foyer in a crouch, ears straining for any sound to give away Cavett's position. A draft of cool air and the sound of pouring rain from outside told him that Cavett had gone outside, likely to make an escape in the car.

Cavett was injured, but the Phantom didn't know how badly or whether he had another gun. He rose slowly from his crouch. One step, two steps, three, pistol at the ready. A flash of lightning, and he saw a dark shape to his right. Cavett hadn't gone outside at all.

Then another flash, this time in the Phantom's head as Cavett swung a heavy table lamp and clubbed his skull. He sank to the floor dazed, and in an instant, Cavett was kneeling on his chest, hands around his throat.

"Baines! Where are you?" It was Spender. The Phantom tried to cry out but Cavett's grip was too strong. Lightning flashed and the Phantom saw Cavett's face for an instant, teeth bared in a rictus of insanity. But Spender could not see him.

In a last effort, the Phantom grabbed a handful of Cavett's beard in one hand and dug his nails into the scar tissue and clawed at the tender flesh under it. Cavett cried out in pain.

Three shots, and Cavett's grip loosened. He fell away from the Phantom, who gulped air convulsively.

"Baines? Did I get him?"

"Yes," the Phantom gasped. "I think so." He lit his lighter, and in its flickering light saw Cavett lying face up on the floor. Two of Spender's shots had missed, but one had struck Cavett in the center of his forehead. "He's dead."

"Thank God." Koch stood in the doorway of the den, a fireplace poker in his hand.

"Candles. Do you have candles?" The Phantom's voice was ragged.

"Yes." Koch disappeared for a moment and returned with a candelabra that lit the scene in grim detail. Cavett's forehead sported a simple hole. The back of his skull had blown out, and blood soaked into the carpet around his head. Koch turned away and unashamedly vomited.

"Don't feel bad, Colin," Spender quipped. "If I had eyes I'd probably puke too."

• • •

The Sheriff arrived soon after with a deputy in tow. Sheriff Bill Flynn was a tall, lean man fellow with a weathered face. "What the hell went on here?"

The Phantom stepped forward. "May I explain, Sheriff?"

"Yeah, I'd like that."

"Your accent. Brooklyn?"

Flynn nodded. "Yeah. Nineteen years on the force and I left to move here where things would be peaceful."

"If you were on the NYPD, then you'll recognize this." The Phantom palmed the tiny jeweled domino mask, a symbol of his identity recognized by law enforcement everywhere.

Flynn's eyes widened. "You're—"

The Phantom nodded. "Yes. I am. Now if you'll sit down with us, I'll tell you the story...."

• • •

In the middle of the Phantom's account, the Sheriff's interrupted him. "Who's that?" he said, leaping to his feet and drawing his revolver.

"It's all right, Sheriff." Koch opened the French window and Luke and Willamette entered. Both were dripping wet, and Luke had his arm tucked into his buttoned coat in lieu of a sling.

"The brakes failed," he said. "We went off the road into the trees. I'm afraid the Packard's a total loss, Mister Spender."

"No matter. I'm just pleased that you're both alive."

Willamette looked relieved to see the Sheriff. "What's happened?"

"Pour yourselves a drink, both of you. Sit and listen." Koch said.

They did and the Sheriff said, "So you and Spender were working this together the whole time?"

"Not exactly," the Phantom said. "I had to keep an open mind as to who the killer might be. But eventually I realized that he wasn't the culprit."

"When did you know that Laszlo was Cavett?"

"A mannerism of his gave him away. When he started the car at the train depot, he cranked the engine a few times before switching on the ignition. It's something pilots do with rotary-cylinder engines because the oil settles in the lower cylinders. I admit I was slow in seeing it, but I was watching a lot of doors at once. I recall from reading the information Spender gave me that Cavett was a pilot in the War."

"So you knew when we were talking upstairs in Masters' room?" Spender said.

"Yes. I let him hear what I wanted him to hear. Cavett stole the blood pressure cuff from the doctor's bag and a few sleeping pills to put in his own coffee. He killed Masters then spiked the coffee and faked unconsciousness to cast suspicion on Doctor Branson. I figured he'd make his play, and I was right."

"You took a big chance," the Sheriff said.

"I had to force his hand. I'm sure he heard the talk about dissolving the tontine before supper and he would have to act quickly before that could happen. Masters and Willamette would split the forty grand and he'd get nothing. What I saw at first was a rational plan. I wasn't factoring madness into the equation. But I was ready for him." He patted the cane.

"I should say 'good riddance,'" Spender said. "But all I can say now is poor devil."

"I agree," said Koch, "but to think he had me fooled for three years." He shuddered involuntarily.

"Well, Anson," Spender said. "Looks as if you get the whole pot."

"I won't refuse it, but what an awful way to come by it."

"Intelligence, plus vengefulness, plus patience, plus madness," the Phantom said. "A deadly mix. Cavett recalled the tontine and realized it was the perfect vehicle to bring you together."

"And he would have succeeded if it weren't for you," Spender said.

"Don't sell yourself short. It was your aim in the dark that brought him down." He pulled his collar away to reveal the bruises on his throat. "Otherwise he might have killed me in the bargain. I guess you could say it was a case of blind justice."

. . .

The orchestra played a lush arrangement of "Body and Soul." Van and Muriel glided around the ballroom floor among the dancers, the tails of his tuxedo coat swaying with the folds of her silken gown.

"Sprezzatura," Muriel said. "That's the word I was trying to think of."

"What's it mean?" Van said, although he already knew the answer.

"Studied carelessness. It's a Renaissance word originally applied to art, but it's expanded a little to include people who work hard at looking as if they aren't. That's how I see your dancing."

"Spoken like a true art major." Van frowned. "Should I be offended?"

"Hardly. It makes me feel flattered that you make such an effort to make me look graceful."

Van laughed. "That you make truly effortless, Muriel."

The song ended and they strolled arm in arm back to their table. The campaign dinner for Assemblyman Charles "Charlie" Grayson was well attended by a Who's Who of New York society. Muriel's father, Frank Havens, was standing at the table with an arm around Mark Spender.

"Muriel, Van," he said, "I want you to meet Mark Spender. His father and I were great friends in college. Mark, this is my daughter Muriel and another of my friends, Richard Curtis Van Loan."

Muriel took his hand first and shook it gently. "How do you do, Mister Spender."

"Please, call me Mark. Your voice is lovely. Melodic." He released her hand and reached for Van's. Spender shook it firmly. "It's a pleasure to meet you Curtis."

"Please, everyone calls me Van."

Spender's eyebrow twitched. "Have we met before?"

"I don't believe so," Van said.

"I never forget a voice." He pulled Van toward him and said, *sotto voce,* "or the very distinctive squeak of a pair of shoes. Still wearing 'Roué, I see. Or rather smell."

Van blinked, startled and drew back a step.

"Orientals have a tradition that if one saves a man's life," Spender said. "The man becomes his responsibility, for whatever wrongs he may do are on the rescuer's head. I agree wholeheartedly."

"Let's hope that if that ever happens," Van said, "you will have made no mistake." The band struck up "I've got a Crush on You." "They're playing our song, Muriel." He turned to Spender and Frank. "If you'll excuse us."

"Of course," Spender said with a smile.

"What was that all about?" Muriel said as they held each other a bit too closely to be casual.

"Beats me," Van said. But in the back of his head he was filing a caution about shoes and the future.

THE END

FRED ADAMS, JR. is a retired Penn State University English Professor who spends his days writing pulp fiction and his nights working as a singer-songwriter. His Sam Dunne novel *Dead Man's Melody* was nominated as Pulp Novel of the Year in 2017's Pulp Factory Awards, and his Smith Brothers novel *The Eye of Quang-Chi* was nominated for the same award in 2018. His titles include *Hitwolf* 1 and 2, *Six Gun Terrors* vols. 1, 2, and 3, and *C.O. Jones: Mobsters and Monsters, Skinners,* and *The Damned and the Doomed.* His original Sherlock Holmes anthology *The Affair of the Chronic Argonaut* was recently published by Pro Se Press. Forthcoming titles from Airship 27 include *C.O. Jones: Home Front, Six Gun Terrors 4: The Town Killers,* a Sam Dunne Mystery, *Blood is the New Black,* and *Holster Full of Death,* a Dead Sheriff novel. He lives in Mount Pleasant, Pennsylvania in "perpetual terror of boredom."

Visit Fred's website at http://drphreddee.com/author

www.ingramcontent.com/pod-product-compliance
Lightning Source LLC
Chambersburg PA
CBHW051142260626
47170CB00005B/1926